BLOOD DEBTS

Leonidas the Gladiator Mysteries

ASHLEY GARDNER

JA/AG Publishing

CHAPTER 1

◆

"THE BAKER OWES US MONEY."

I crawled out of sleep when a slim stick tapped my side and a woman's voice slid through my dreams. Cassia had learned to use the stick to poke at me, because I usually came roaring awake, ready to murder all within reach.

When she'd first come to live with me, Cassia had shaken me from a dream in which I'd been surrounded by swords, the ghosts of men I'd slain rising up to drag me down. I'd been naked and without weapons, only my balled fists for defense.

I'd grabbed the arm that had come at me and torn open my eyes to find Cassia in terror, her slender wrist in my deadly grip. I'd nearly broken her arm before I'd let go.

Hence, the stick.

I was too exhausted this morning for roaring, so I mumbled, "Wha'?"

"The baker." Cassia returned the polished branch of walnut to the corner and picked up the wax tablet on which she did the household accounts, such as they were. "Quintus Publius. You guarded his shipments from Ostia three weeks ago, and he has yet to pay a thing. He owes us ten sestertii."

"Mmph." I scrubbed my face, hoping to sink back into darkness. "Send him a notice." I settled my head on my hard pillow. "You like to send notices."

"I have sent him seventeen," Cassia said crisply. "He ignores them. You ought to go yourself. He will not be able to ignore *you*."

I opened my eyes all the way. Cassia sat in her usual place, a stool on the other side of our one-roomed apartment, near the door. She wore a modest sheath of a dress, sandals I'd bought her, and held her stylus poised over her tablet. I always thought of her like that, eyes on the hinged wooden and wax tablet in her hand, stylus at the ready to add a notation.

Her black hair, pulled up out of her face, curled wildly about her forehead and cascaded down her back in one tail. No hairdresser had styled those curls— Cassia was a slave, bestowed upon me by my unknown benefactor, a man who'd apparently followed my career in the arena more ardently than I had.

This man, whoever he was, had decided I needed looking after, and sent Cassia to be my caretaker when I'd gained my freedom six months ago. Cassia had grown up the daughter of a slave, who'd been a scribe to a very wealthy patrician family in Campania. She was here now because, after her father's death, the master of the house had decided to notice that Cassia had become a woman, and Cassia's mistress had made certain she was quickly sold.

Cassia didn't know who our benefactor was either. Everything went through another scribe, a dried stick of a slave called Hesiodos, who steadfastly refused to tell us.

Cassia dressed her hair simply, because she wasn't good at hair, she'd told me, or clothes, or cooking, or really much of anything else, which was why no one had known what to do with her once her father had gone to the gods. Her master had known what he wanted, and so Cassia's mistress had ejected her.

What Cassia excelled at was accounts. And noticing things, important things. And driving a man spare so he couldn't sleep.

These days, I liked sleep. There was no reason to pull myself out of bed—no training, no meals of barley and vegetables, or grand feasts in my honor the night before the games. These feasts had always been wasted on me because I could never swallow a bite.

"Tomorrow." I closed my eyes, seeking the comfort of oblivion.

Often the dreams broke through to haunt me, but sometimes there was nothing. Sweet peace. I must not have slept at all in the seven years I was a gladiator because now I could not get enough of it.

"Leonidas." Cassia's firm voice broke that peace.

This time I came up with a hint of a snarl. *"Wha'?"*

"If the baker pays us, we can remain in our palatial surroundings. Otherwise, we'll be out on the street. And hungry. We can prevent this by prying what we are owed out of Quintus."

The interesting thing about our so-called bene-factor is that he didn't pay our rent or provide us food. He'd found me this apartment, bestowed upon me a slave no one else wanted, and then left the rest of our living up to us. What this man would demand in return for this uneven generosity remained to be seen.

Cassia trailed off, watching to gauge the effect of her words on me, every one of them reasonable, every one unarguable.

The trouble with Cassia was that she was nearly always right. A man needed money to live. A gladiator in a ludus did not, but I was no longer kept at others' expense. The animal, freed from its cage, didn't know how to hunt.

My hint of a snarl turned into a real one as I hauled myself up and off the slab of wood our landlord called a bed. The blanket Cassia must have laid over me in the night slid from my bare body as I rose to my feet. Cassia averted her gaze, her cheeks burning red.

I'd never met a woman shy with men before, one who didn't openly size up the goods, especially when they took up half the apartment. But then, my experi-ence with women had been in brothels and with those eager to sneak themselves into a gladiator's cell. Cassia had lived with modest women who'd covered them-selves at all times and required her to as well.

Cassia's head remained bent, her eyes fixed reso-lutely on her tablet. Maybe she'd caught sight of a mistake in her calculations. No, Cassia didn't make mistakes. She was simply uncomfortable with so much naked flesh in such a small space.

I'd never noticed my own body much until Cassia's

arrival. I'd thought of male bodies in terms of places to stab—chest for heart and lungs, abdomen for guts, throat for a rapid kill. Women's bodies were somewhat different—their parts fit with mine for a short time of mind-numbing pleasure to chase away the demons.

Cassia, on the other hand, saw *me*, Leonidas, the whole person. No one else ever had. Instead of being flattered, I always felt the immediate need to cover myself.

I reached for a tunic and pulled it on. Cassia flicked me a glance, and she breathed out, no mistaking her relief.

I pretended to ignore her while I sluiced clean water from the ewer over my face and looked around for my sandals. There they were, my one pair, in a neat line by the door. Cassia tidied every night after I went to bed—if collapsing onto my mat of reeds on a wooden block could be given such a formal term.

"Not that tunic," Cassia said behind me. I felt her critical eyes on my back. "A clean one."

I halted. No wonder Jupiter constantly fled Juno. She was probably always going on at him about wearing clean tunics and combing his hair.

I'd forgotten—clean tunic on the peg, dirty one on the floor for Cassia to take to the laundry.

As I put my hand on the fabric at the back of my neck, ready to pull off the offending garment, Cassia said, "No, no, on second thought, you ought to wear that. The wine stain from last night's meal is the exact color of blood. It makes you look as though you wrestled someone into submission. He'll pay up like a lamb."

No gladiator, no matter how much in fear of his life, had ever been as ruthless as Cassia when someone owed her money. Owed *me* money, I should say. I did the jobs, she kept note of them, and then sent me to bully those who didn't pay.

Cassia wasn't wrong, though. We needed the cash or we wouldn't eat or have anywhere to sleep. I was bad at the basics of life, Cassia was good at it, and so we went along.

I settled the tunic without a word, smoothed my hand over my close-cropped hair, and ducked out into the morning sun.

I'd managed to block out the noise and brightness of the Roman morning while I'd slept, but now they both hit me full force.

Cassia and I lived one floor above the shop of a wine merchant at the base of the Quirinal. It might have been cheaper for us to live in an insula, but I had a horror of those huge blocks of buildings made to house so many living beings. They fell down on occasion, burying all within them. Our apartment had been built for the wine-seller's mother-in-law, standing empty after she'd passed. We had one rectangular room and a balcony that was nothing more than the flat roof of the wine shop below.

The street flowed with activity. The current of men in tunics—a few with togas—swept past the wine shop with its amphorae resting in rows neat enough for Cassia's approval, drawing me with them into the pulsing heat of Rome.

My route today took me past the forum of Augustus, the emperor and god, whom even I'd heard of.

Elderly men in the baths would reminisce about how wonderful Rome had been in the golden age of Augustus, and how we'd never see its like again.

From what Cassia told me, we now had more bath houses, a greater abundance of clean water, wares from every corner of the empire, and more relative peace than in the time of Augustus, but I'd noticed that the more gray hair a man had, the more nostalgic he became. Cassia also pointed out that these men could only have been tiny children when Augustus died, and would hardly remember life under his rule.

My steps turned me toward the Subura, an area that ran along the base of the Quirinal and Viminal hills. Smoke coated the air because of the fires perpetually burning to heat the baths for the day. The aqueducts that provided water for baths and every fountain in the city stalked along the tops of the hills above me.

I heard my name on occasion as I walked under the colonnade that shaded the street. This was usual as I moved about Rome — my fights in the amphitheatres had been celebrated. But if I turned aside to speak to every person who hailed me, I'd never reach my destination. I wouldn't mind, but if I didn't return soon with the money, Cassia would give me her sorrowful look and make another note on her tablet.

"It's him," I heard a man exclaim. "Leonidas!"

"Where?" another responded. "No, it isn't. You're daft."

"Yes, it is. That was him. I saw the scar."

The scar in question cut along the base of my throat and down into my tunic. If the cut had landed with the force intended, my blood would have spilled in a swift torrent, and I would have died on the arena sand. My own strike had lessened the blow, and the other man had died instead.

I am called Leonidas because my lanista, a man who bought and trained gladiators, said I fought with the intensity of Leonidas the Spartan king and his men at Thermopylae. Thus, Leonidas the Gladiator was born. Since I'd been eager to shuck my old name, which had only brought me trouble, I didn't object. Leonidas I became at age eighteen, and so I remained.

"Leonidas!" The last voice was very young, very eager, and fearing disappointment. "Look!"

I turned my head. A grubby boy stood in the shadow of an archway, holding up a terra cotta cup for me to see. The side of the cup bore a crude sketch of a man who could have been anyone, except for the scratched letters that spelled out, *Leonidas*. I recognized the word, because it was the only one I knew how to read.

At this man's feet was sprawled a second gladiator, his fallen trident beside him. The one Greek letter I knew, theta, was scratched beneath him, meaning the man on the ground was dead.

Hot wind swept down the street. With it came the scent of sand, blood, sweat, and the metallic tang of the inside of my helmet. I couldn't see the thousands surrounding me in the amphitheatre, but I could hear them. The roar of voices, the chant of my name. *Le-o-ni-das*. The press of air and heat sent sweat trickling down my bare back and legs.

A rush of fear, rage, and desperation came at me, swirling away the packed streets of Rome. I seemed to look through the grill of my eye pieces, the helmet a cage, and saw the trident come at my midsection. A shout left my mouth as I barreled it aside with my elbow, the trident's point glancing off my helmet. In another second, the man was down, the crowd screaming for his death. *Iugula! Kill him!*

Sweat poured down my body as air raked my lungs. Someone brushed past me, and my vision swam back. A lower-class woman surrounded by her friends on their way to the market parted to flow around me. The gaggle of them laughed together, the soft fabric of a fluttering skirt brushing my ankles.

As the fog began to clear, I crouched down in front of the boy. He was somewhere between five and maybe eight summers, skinny with poverty, teeth half gone, hair brittle and lank. His tunic was threadbare, sandals held on with twine.

Somehow he'd found the money to buy the piece of junk he held, showing one of my forgotten bouts from years ago. I'd forgotten none of them.

I wanted to dash the cup to the ground, tell him to spend his money on better things, but the boy held the cup as though it were precious gold.

Cassia's voice buzzed like a fly at the back of my skull. *Whatever did you do that for, Leonidas? You could at least have given him the price for it, poor lad.*

I touched the cup. "It was hot that day," I said. "The amphitheatre in that town was gravelly, and we had to wear sandals. I had grit in my shoes."

The boy's eyes widened in fascination.

"He fought well," I went on, tracing the fallen body of the man who'd called himself Dionysius. "I was lucky to win. Was almost skewered by the trident a couple of times."

The boy listened, open-mouthed, dark eyes round with wonder. To him, the fight was a legend. To me, it had been just another day at the games.

I fished a copper coin from the pouch at my waist and dropped it into the cup. "Go tell the fruit seller to give you his best for that—tell him I sent you."

The boy nodded, his eyes and mouth no less round. I rose and shooed him off. He scampered away, his head high, joy in his step.

I was that boy once—the memory tapped me out of nowhere. Had nothing and no one, only a few precious things to keep me from complete despair. I watched him bob along until he was lost among the crowd, swallowed by Rome's million inhabitants.

The baker's shop was around the next corner, built a little way from the end of a row of shops, an open counter in front where the baker did business. Ovens fired in the back, the wall above them pocked with round holes where the bread taken from the ovens would cool.

I'd come at a lull in the baker's day. His morning bread would have been finished and fetched by the women or household slaves of this area, giving him time to bake other things to sell, or perhaps doze under the counter.

Quintus was awake, however, puttering about, a small, bald man in a tunic and sandals. He was wiry, every muscle tight from shoveling bread into and out of ovens all day, his back a bit hunched from the same.

I said nothing as I approached the concrete slab of

the counter, noting that the mosaic on the top depicted sea creatures, nothing to do with bread or baking.

I leaned my hands on the counter and waited. Quintus shoved himself halfway into a roaring oven and came back out with an empty paddle and not so much as a burn or singed hair.

"Yes?" he asked impatiently as he turned around. "You'll have to—"

He halted in mid-word, his parted lips showing me brownish teeth in blackening gums. He snapped this mouth shut and swallowed. "Leonidas."

I could not have been a welcome sight. I stood two feet taller than the baker and was twice as broad. The famous scar that trailed down my neck symbolized my defeat of death. My hands, now fists, were as big as the stones he used for grinding seeds to paste.

Quintus looked so terrified I feared he'd drop dead on the spot. Cassia would be most put out if I let him die—we'd likely never get paid.

"It's Cassia," I said, making my tone apologetic. "She likes her accounts to balance."

Quintus gulped. "She is Greek," he said, as though that explained it.

Desperate, I could have told him. Cassia had a horror of being on the street, wretched and homeless, a dangerous situation that could end quickly in defilement and death.

I tried to feel the same fear and could not. I hadn't felt anything in a long, long while.

For Cassia's sake, I was here, badgering a man who thought he'd gotten away with not paying his debt to the second most dangerous man in Rome. That was what I'd heard people call me. I assumed they believed the princeps, Nero, to be the first.

"I'll take half," I said. "That should keep her quiet for a while." I sent Quintus a look that suggested we had to do what was necessary to keep the women who ran our lives happy.

He wet his lips. "I don't have it." His face was bright red, whether because he lied or told the truth and was afraid of it, I could not say. "I swear to you, I don't have it. I don't even have half. But ..."

Quintus trailed off, his flush fading as something like relief took over. "Gaius Selenius owes me money. Quite a bit of it. Part of the shipment you guarded from Ostia was his—I moved it at my own expense. If you go along and pry the money out of *him*, I can pay you. And a few coins extra for your trouble."

I smothered a sigh. A disadvantage to being one of the most famous gladiators of the day, even as a *veteres*, was that other men expected me to do their dirty deeds for them. *Rough up a man who insulted me. Find a man who owes me money, and we'll all get paid.*

The fact that Quintus hadn't gone after the money owed himself meant that Selenius frightened him. Selenius might be surrounded by bodyguards or have a vicious disposition, more inclined to have a small man beaten than pay his debt to him. What luck that I'd come along this morning.

But there was nothing for it. Unless I turned the baker upside down and shook him, I would not return with money today. The thought of facing Cassia empty-handed was not a happy one.

"Where is this Gaius Selenius?" I asked, resigned.

Quintus brightened. "On the Clivus Suburanus, in a *macellum* near the Porticus Liviae. His shop is in the middle of the market, by the atrium. He's a money-changer."

Better and better. Money-changers were a despised class of men, lumped with usurers and tax collectors. Even gladiators, though we were *infamis*, at the very bottom of society, had higher reputations.

I abruptly turned from Quintus without a farewell or another word, joining the crowds in the increasing heat of the day. Once the sun hit its zenith, in the sixth hour, shops would close, business would halt, and men and women alike would wander to the baths, to meals, to lounge in the shade and wait for evening. I'd go back to sleep.

Once in the street, I turned down a winding lane toward the Clivus Suburanus. The twisting sway was so narrow I could lift my arms and touch walls on either side, and still my elbows would be bent. Despite the stink of refuse that curled in my nose, the tall, crammed-together buildings in this passageway shaded me from the blazing sun.

At the end of this lane, I turned into a wider, airy street of shops that were doing a brisk business. A tavern served food and drink to plenty of people who'd found time to stop and ingest barley and beans, soup and pork.

All manner of things were sold on this street—silk cloth from the east, spices and peppers, clay lamps and pots, fruits and vegetables, fresh flowers, sandals, and the baskets to carry it all in. A person could clothe himself, get his dinner, light his house and decorate it, buy his bedding, and purchase a pot for his slops, without ever having to turn a corner.

I'd lived most of my life in this city, first snatching survival in the streets, then in prison, then in the ludus. The lanista didn't lock us in; we were free to move about and take odd jobs in the city, as long as we were back in our cells at dusk.

But I hadn't really seen the place until I'd emerged from the ludus a free man. The city had gained a new tint, the stones a golden glow, the hills a grandeur. Even the fires that constantly burned gave it a scent that I'd come to associate with my home.

I turned at last to the Clivus Suburanus and found the passage leading to the *macellum* — an indoor market-place housed within a large building. I ducked in, following the baker's directions.

This *macellum* was owned by a patrician who prob-ably lived in a villa in the hills. He'd turned his prop-erty into rental spaces for sellers of food and other goods. The main building had shops around all of the outer walls and a few in the middle near the atrium. I had been here before — thick walls and the arched roof kept out the heat, which made it a popular place.

A niche in a wall inside the main door held a terra cotta carving of an erect phallus, a symbol of fertility — five times the size of any man's prick and correct in every detail. It was customary to give such statues around the city a rub for good fortune. I gave this one a pat in passing, both for luck and in hopes of sympa-thetic magic. My phallic instrument had been sleeping as much as I had lately.

The *macellum* was quieter than usual, only a few

slaves in tunics buying wares for whatever household they worked for. Two were Gauls, with very pale hair and blue eyes, wooden baskets on their arms to hold what they purchased for their master or mistress. They were big men, muscular and tall. I was taller than most Roman men, which made people question my ancestry, but these two both topped me by an inch.

They stopped and stared at me as I went by. They might have recognized me from the games or they thought me as unusual as I thought them.

The two slaves finished their transaction across the counter of the stall nearest the main entrance, a vendor of *garum*, the smelly fermented fish sauce that made Cassia blench.

As I reached the inner shops near the atrium, all was quiet. It was nearly midday, and most of the vendors in here had already shut down, slipping away home for a nap or to the baths to relax.

Selenius had one of the innermost shops, a square room with a door on one side, and a counter on another, which could be closed off by a series of vertical wooden boards stuck into slots in the counter and locked in place with iron bars. Other shops had already put in their boards, guarding whatever was inside from casual thieves until they opened the next day.

I was relieved to see Selenius's shop still open. The sooner I made him give over Quintus's money, the sooner I could drop our earnings in front of Cassia and resume my sleep.

The mosaic tiles on his counter spelled out words, possibly that this was the place of Selenius. I glanced about for bodyguards but saw none. I didn't like that. A man who dealt in coins, counting out Roman ones in exchange for whatever people in the far-flung corners of the world used for money, had to be cautious. Coins ran the Roman Empire, and everyone wanted them.

Selenius didn't appear to be here either. I wondered if someone had run ahead and warned him I was coming. If so, he'd left his shop open to all who might traipse through at this quiet hour.

There wasn't much light inside the shop. The only illumination came through the square hole in the exact center of the building, which lit the atrium, much like it would in a rich man's private house.

I could see nothing in the shadows over the counter, so I walked to the open door that would let Selenius in and out, and peered inside.

The shop was about ten feet wide on a side, perhaps ten feet high, a perfect cube. There was another door, I saw from this point, a shorter one that presumably led to the shop next door.

I noted a long bench, which Selenius would set outside when he was open for business—the inside of the shop was for storage and safeguarding his stock-piles of coin. I saw no coin, however, but it likely had been taken away and locked up for the day.

As I ran my gaze over the space, it came to rest on a man lying in an unmoving huddle under the counter. His face, head, hands, legs, and long tunic were soaked with blood, and blood had spread in a puddle that stopped shy of the doorway where I stood. A black line ran across his throat, and his eyes were fixed in frozen terror.

I stood in silence, looking down at the man, trying to feel horror, dismay, fear … but there was nothing. I remained unmoving, as though the entire world had come to a halt, until a small noise made me jerk my head up.

The door across the shop had opened. A boy stood on the threshold, a small lad clutching a cup with my name etched on it. He gaped over the blood at me, eyes wide, and then he dropped the cup, which shattered into the crimson pool at his feet.

CHAPTER 2

"STAY THERE," I SAID IN A HARD VOICE.

The boy remained frozen in place, his chest moving with his sharp intake of breath.

I backed out of the doorway I stood in and strode rapidly to the next shop. I reasoned it must be unlocked if the boy had come through it, but it was not. The boards had been fixed in place above the counter, the iron bars firmly run through rings in the boards and into the stone walls. No opening under the counter or around the side of the wall held any crevice that would admit a small boy. Then how had he gotten in?

I returned to Selenius's stall, the boy obediently waiting. Terrified, he still followed the orders of Leonidas, champion of the games.

I stepped carefully around the pool of blood, the stink of it making my vision blur. I sucked in deep breaths through my mouth, willing my thoughts to

remain in the present, and skirted the blood to reach
the boy.

"How did you get here?" I demanded.

He pointed to the black opening of the door behind
him. I couldn't see where it went but a noisome smell
leeched from the shadows.

I glanced at the man on the floor—I assumed he
was Selenius, though I'd never met him. The blood
came not from many injuries but from the large one
across his throat. The vessels in his neck had been
severed, and blood had poured forth to kill him
quickly.

Whoever had done this had known exactly where
to cut. It was the sort of execution a soldier would
know how to perform—or a gladiator.

Very little frightened me anymore, but the thought
of being tried for another murder, found guilty, and
tossed back into the arena filled me with slow dread.
Quintus the baker had sent me here—had he known
Selenius lay dead and hoped I'd be taken for the crime?

I thought of Quintus's polished face and ingenuous
dark eyes, which I swore had no guile in them, apart
from avoiding payment of my fee. He might be as igno-
rant of this death as I'd been.

No matter what, we couldn't linger. The boy had
stooped to the fragments of his precious cup. I pushed
his hands away, not wanting him to cut himself on the
shards, but I gathered every single one of them. Put
together, they had my name on them, and I wanted no
connection in anyone's mind between dead Selenius
and Leonidas the Gladiator.

I shoved the fragments into the pouch at my belt and leaned down to lift the boy. Before I could, he grabbed one more piece from the floor, and then I hefted him into my arms.

He weighed next to nothing, bones in a threadbare tunic.

I decided not to ask where he lived. If I carried him home, people would remember—I could not move a step in this city without it being remarked upon.

It would be the talk of every supper for days to come if I were seen walking about the city with a small boy under my arm. I couldn't hide him under a convenient toga, because ex-gladiators, freedmen who were barely human, didn't wear them.

"Where does that lead?" I pointed through the doorway behind him.

"Down," was the helpful reply.

He'd come in here, so he must be able to get out. I ducked with him through the doorway to find a brick-lined passage that soon grew very dark. I smelled waste, human and animal, which meant this tunnel probably went to a maintenance hatch to the sewers. Rome was pockmarked with shafts that led to the considerable network of tunnels and sewers that crawled to every corner of Rome.

The boy was much smaller than I was—I hoped he didn't expect me to slither through tiny orifices in the bowels of Rome. It would be a stupid death for me to get stuck in an opening with the city's waste flushing through it to drown me.

I set the lad on his feet but kept hold of his hand. "Show me," I said as I closed the door behind us.

He started off at a rapid pace, dragging me down low-ceilinged tunnels, my skin scraping on the walls as I staggered along.

We twisted and eventually plunged downward, the stone floor sloping inward from the walls, but not to the sewers as I'd feared. The last passage ended in a rough set of steps that led down to a wooden door.

I carefully opened this door and peered out.

It took me a moment to gain my bearings. We were at the base of the Esquiline Hill, near the area called the Figlinae, where potters had their factories. The street before me was lined with shops, this obscure narrow door obviously for maintenance purposes. People thronged here as they did everywhere, barely noticing us as we emerged from a battered door in a wall of shops and warehouses to blend in with them.

A short walk took us to the fountain of Orpheus at a broad crossroads, where a marble Orpheus tried to tame stone animals with his lyre. We turned here and journeyed back through the Subura to the Forum Augusti, where I lost hold of the boy's hand in the crush of people.

In three steps I caught up to him and lifted him into my arms. The boy never struggled or cried out, didn't protest or question. He simply rode against my chest, sanguine that his hero Leonidas held him.

I hefted him around the corner toward the wine shop, and then took the wooden stairs two at a time, to burst through the door into our apartment.

Cassia looked up from the tablets and scrolls that surrounded her, her pen falling from her fingers in surprise. She leapt to her feet, one scroll rolling up on itself and spattering ink, as I lowered the boy to his feet and shut the door.

"This is Cassia," I said to the boy. "She'll take care of you."

I had the pleasure of seeing Cassia, who always knew what to say at every occasion, at a loss for words. She opened her mouth, switched her stare to the lad, closed her mouth, and looked back at me.

"Who—?"

"I don't know," I cut her off. "I found him. Or, he found me. The money-changer is dead—Quintus sent me to collect a debt from him, but he's dead. Someone killed him."

I spit out the explanation as swiftly as possible, my entire body willing me to walk across the room and collapse upon my bed. I'd sleep and let Cassia sort it all out. When she'd finished, she'd wake me and tell me what to do.

Her mouth hung open again, showing even white teeth against her red tongue. She moved her gaze to the boy, who had put his fingers to his lower lip and watched her apprehensively.

"Killed?" she repeated in a faint voice.

"Murdered, butchered, his throat sliced. Professional." I moved my arm as though I cut across a man's throat. "I came here. I told no one."

As I spoke, I untied my pouch from my belt and shook the fragments of terra cotta onto the table. Cassia touched them, mystified.

"Give me the piece you picked up," I said to the boy. "Cassia can stick this together for you again."

Cassia turned over the shard that had *Leonidas* scratched on it, and her lips formed an *O*.

The boy opened his fist and dropped what he held onto the table. It wasn't a fragment, or even pottery, but a small roll of papyrus.

Cassia snatched it up and smoothed it out, her eyes widening as she studied the spidery writing within. She sat down, her interest caught, her entire body growing animated as it did when something intrigued her.

"Where did he find this?" she asked without looking up.

"At Selenius's shop," I said. "I thought he'd picked up another piece of the cup."

"No." Cassia turned the paper around and held it up to me as though I'd be astonished by it. Then she seemed to remember I couldn't read a word and laid it back down. "It's a voucher. For a traveling patron to change for Roman coin."

I didn't respond. When Cassia began speaking like a scribe I gave up following her. I crouched down by the boy who was torn between bewilderment and fascination.

"What's your name, lad?"

The boy took his fingers out of his mouth. "Sergius."

I waited, but he said nothing more. I didn't know if that was his praenomen or his family or clan name. He might have had no other if he was a boy from the streets. What if he was from a brothel?

My chest burned. I'd gone to brothels ever since I'd figured out what my wick was for, and as a gladiator I'd been a welcome guest — my lanista paid for the best.

I favored women only, fully grown ones, that is, but there were plenty of Romans who indulged in young men; for some, the younger the better.

Lads and girls Sergius's age would have no choice but to fulfill the indulgence. They weren't old enough to seek a living elsewhere, and likely their parents had sold them to the brothels when they couldn't afford to feed them.

The children in these places were hollow-eyed and broken, knowing they could not protest or stop anything the customers wanted to do to them. I'd noticed the relief on their faces whenever I walked past them for the women who actually had breasts and hips.

I'd not been able to do a damn thing to help them. I had been owned myself at the time, and now I barely had enough to keep me and Cassia fed. I hadn't been back to the brothels in a long time.

But I'd sacrifice to any god willing to listen to keep this little lad away from them—a boy whose only delight was a cheap cup with my name on it.

"Do you have a family?" I asked him.

Sergius considered this and then shook his head.

"Where do you live then?"

"With Alba."

Since any number of women in the empire could be called Alba, this didn't help much.

"Is she your mother?"

A shake of his head, a faint distaste that I'd even think so.

"Mistress of a brothel?" I asked.

A nod. That clinched the matter. He'd not be returning to Alba.

"Did she send you on an errand today?" I continued.

Another nod.

"And what was this errand?"

"Fish sauce. Then I saw you."

Cassia had lifted her head to listen, her elbows on the table as she held the small piece of papyrus between her fingers.

"And you followed me," I said. "After I left the baker's."

Sergius gave me a single nod. "Took a shortcut."

Interesting. "How did you know where I was going?"

"I heard Quintus tell you to go to Selenius. I ran to get there first."

"And what did you see?"

Horror crept into his eyes. "Saw him dead."

"That was Selenius, was it?"

Sergius nodded vigorously. "Didn't like him. Mean. Ugly. Stank."

He hadn't smelled that good dead either. "You knew him?"

"Saw him about when I went to the market for Alba. He had his slave kick me if I came too close to his bench. Once he knocked me down."

My anger at Selenius bloomed, no matter the man was dead.

The small slip of papyrus fluttered between Cassia's fingers, distracting me. I eyed it in irritation. "What is that? Explain in words I will understand."

Cassia laid down the paper and smoothed it out,

taking on the patient look she did whenever she had to teach me something.

"When a man from the outreaches of the empire decides to travel to the city of Rome, he will need money. But it is dangerous to walk the roads with a box full of coins if one does not have armed body-guards every step of the way. Therefore, a man can go to a merchant or shipping agent who is part of a business in Rome, pay a certain amount of money, and obtain a voucher. When he reaches Rome, he takes the voucher to a shipping agent of the same company, who will then give him the amount he paid in. A small fee is involved, of course, but this way, a man can travel and not risk being robbed of all he has in the world."

A clever arrangement—*if* the man didn't lose his voucher and if he could be reasonably certain he'd get his money back at the other end.

"Selenius wasn't a shipping agent," I pointed out.

"Some money-changers honor the vouchers," Cassia said. "If they have an arrangement with the shipping company. Money-changers have plenty of coins, don't they?"

"All right then, this Selenius was a man travelers visited to collect on their vouchers," I said, making certain I'd followed her explanation. "What of it?"

Even ordinary transactions excited Cassia's heart, but this did not explain her elation over the slip of paper.

"This voucher is a bit different." Cassia held it up again, smiling hugely. "This one is a forgery."

CHAPTER 3

I STARED AT THE PAPER SHE WAVED BUT WAS NO more enlightened than before.

"How do you know that?"

Cassia laid the sheet neatly on the table next to the broken cup. "When I was in the household of Glaucia Rufina, I traveled extensively with her. It was my task to go to the shipping agents and money-changers and pay in and take out. I kept track of all the finances." She trailed off.

She meant before Glaucia Rufina's husband had laid his hands on Cassia, and Cassia, once a trusted slave with many privileges, found herself banished.

Now she kept accounts for me. My finances were a fly to the elephant of those of a lady like Glaucia Rufina, but Cassia kept them with the same efficiency. She never complained about the difference in amount except when there wasn't enough to feed us or pay the rent. I'd realized that Cassia liked figures, any figures, didn't matter how large or small. As long as she had numbers to play with, she was content.

"I've handled many of these, some from this very man Gaius Selenius," Cassia said. "This is neatly done. Selenius decorates his with a symbol derived from his mark, so that all will know it's his. There has been an attempt to copy the mark, but it's not quite right. As I say, though, very neatly done. Most people would be fooled." She sounded admiring.

"Why kill him for it?"

Cassia shrugged. "It might have nothing to do with his death. What did you do when you found him? Did you tell anyone?"

"No." I glanced at Sergius, who had lost interest in the conversation and was looking about the apartment in curiosity.

Cassia's eyes widened as she followed my gaze. "You don't think …?" She swallowed, turning back to me in consternation. "You said you thought it was professional."

"I don't know." I balled my fists. "Might have been professional. Or luck."

A frightened person could slice a knife across another's neck and kill him without much effort. The human body was a fragile thing. Trainers, as well as the physicians who'd patched us up, had showed us every single vulnerable point on a man's body and how to stab them to bring about his swift end.

Cassia's dark eyes began to sparkle as they did when she was interested in a thing. I watched her run through scenarios and calculate their likelihood with lightning rapidity. I could do such a thing when it came to a fight, although it was best to let my training take over and not think very hard. Cassia could evaluate a dozen problems from what to eat for breakfast to who might have murdered a money-changer in the time most people could think to wonder what the weather was like.

"You must report it," Cassia said abruptly. "The baker knows you went to Selenius. He sent you. Did others see you near Selenius's shop?"

I told her about the few people who'd been left in the *macellum*, including the two Gauls who'd been finishing their business with the *garum* vendor.

"When someone finds Selenius dead, they will remember Leonidas the Gladiator walking in and then vanishing." Cassia's cheeks lost color, and she twisted her fingers together as she did when she was particularly worried.

"Leonidas, who knows how to kill," I finished for her. This was not the first time someone had connected me, a professional murderer, with a death. "The baker could have known Selenius was dead—he sent me to discover him and to be taken for the murder, so he wouldn't have to pay our be-damned fee." I paused. "I'm sorry I didn't get your money, Cassia. I should have shaken it out of him."

"Never mind about the money." Cassia sprang up and came to my side. She didn't touch me but she stood close enough that I felt the warmth of her stola. "You cannot be accused of this crime. You did not commit it."

I was stunned by two things: First, Cassia saying the words *Never mind about the money*. The second was her stout belief that I had not killed the man. She could not possibly know whether I had gone into the deserted shop of Gaius Selenius, taken all his money, and slit his throat. She hadn't been there, couldn't have seen.

But she believed in me, had from the day she'd met me.

That is, from the moment she'd realized I wouldn't set upon her, ravish her, beat her, and throw her into a corner as she'd fully expected. I'd only asked her what she wanted for dinner.

"If they come for me," I said slowly. "How do I prove I did not kill him?"

Cassia took a step back and surveyed me with calm assessment. "You haven't a drop of blood on you. *That* is a wine stain." She pointed at the purplish splash on the side of my tunic. "You don't even have blood on your shoes—you must have stepped carefully."

I nodded. I had, not wanting to touch what had poured from Selenius's throat.

"Was the blood liquid?" Cassia asked. "Still flowing? Or dried?"

I had a good memory for details, which Cassia had once told me she admired. This surprised me, as I hadn't thought it any sort of special trick. She'd responded that she wrote everything down because she *didn't* have a good memory. I'd had to think on that for a while.

I brought to mind Selenius's wide-open eyes, the blackening gash on his pale neck, the red pool of blood. "Somewhere in between. No longer flowing. Patches shining here and there. Selenius's face was gray."

"Which means he died some time before you arrived. Not a long time, or the blood would be completely dried. It would have helped if you'd touched his body and could tell me whether it was cold or not, but no matter. How long did it take you to reach the shop from the baker's?"

I had little idea of time other than morning, noon, and evening. I could barely make out a sundial, and there hadn't been one conveniently along my route.

"I walked to the baker's from here," I said. "I stopped when Sergius showed me his cup, and then I reached Quintus. Spoke to him for only a few moments. Walked straight from there to Selenius's shop on the Clivus Suburanus, not long before the fountain of Orpheus."

Cassia nodded as she no doubt calculated exactly how many strides I'd taken and how soon that had put me at the *macellum*. She was very good at such reckonings. I'd come to believe she could tell the legions exactly how far they could march every day on the supplies they had and still have energy for battle.

Cassia moved to the table and lifted one of her many wax tablets. "You left here at the beginning of the fifth hour," she said. "I'd say it took you about a quarter of an hour from the baker's to Selenius's." She marked a note. "From the state of his blood, Selenius might have been killed a half hour to an hour before you arrived. That can save you, if a competent physician examines the body and Quintus will agree you were talking to him at the time we say. As you had no notion who Selenius was before Quintus mentioned him, there was no reason for you to kill him before you visited the baker." She sank to her stool as she made her notes, then she tapped the stylus to her lips. "This would clear Quintus as well. He was putting bread in the oven as you arrived, you say, and that's a tricky business. The dough has to rise to a certain point but no further or it's ruined. He'd have to be there to shovel it into the oven at the crucial moment."

Cassia could not cook—she knew the theory of cooking, baking, beer brewing, wine making, and many other crafts of food, but she could not execute any of these herself. We bought all our meals from the tavern down the street.

"That means the boy didn't do it either," I said in a low voice. Sergius had wandered to the corner where my bed was, and now pulled back the shutter to look down into the street. "He followed me to the baker's."

"Unless he did it before you saw him the first time," Cassia pointed out. "Though that's unlikely. I see no blood on him either. Dirt, yes. Whoever cares for him doesn't bathe him." She shook her head in disapproval.

Cassia was always clean, from the toes that peeped from her sandals to the curls on top of her head. She bathed every afternoon and came home smelling of scented oil. I believe one reason she didn't complain about being a slave to a gladiator is that I did not hinder her leaving for the baths at the eighth hour of every day precisely.

"I'm not taking him back to the brothel."

"I agree. Poor lad." Cassia set her stylus on the table. "Where *will* you take him?"

We both knew he could not stay here. We barely had the coin to feed ourselves, in spite of our "benefactor." Cassia tirelessly worked to uncover his identity, but she'd so far not been successful.

I thought in silence then said, "Marcella."

Cassia's brows rose. "Widow of your friend, who has five children of her own?"

"She is kind and always needs help on the farm."

Marcella had been the wife of a gladiator who'd called himself Xerxes. I never learned his real name — I don't think he remembered it. He'd been *secundus palus* at our gladiator school, the second-best fighter. The *primus palus*, the top fighter, had been me. Many commented on the irony of our names — Xerxes the Persian and beaten down Leonidas the Spartan at the Battle of Thermopylae — but we only stared at those who mentioned it until they quietly slunk away.

Xerxes, probably the closest friend I'd had in life, had married and produced five children, even though he'd returned to the ludus every day for training and to the arenas for the games. He'd never been paired with me, and that fact had eventually gotten him killed. If I'd been his opponent that fatal day, I'd have let him win. I'd had nothing to lose — he'd had everything.

Marcella had been grateful to me for returning his body, along with his meager belongings. I'd contributed some of my winnings to help her set up a monument to him with a long inscription she'd told me said what a good husband and father he'd been. Xerxes, dead at age twenty-six.

Cassia watched me a moment and then simply went back to studying the false voucher, which told me she approved of what I wanted to do.

"Can you mend this?" I asked, stirring the shards of the cup with my finger.

Cassia switched her gaze to it, considering. "I believe so. I'll go to the potters' yard and find some paste."

She'd likely have it fixed better than new, or talk the potters into doing it for her. I held out my hand to Sergius. "Come with me."

Sergius looked around from where he held the shutter open, letting in a chunk of hot sunlight. His eyes filled with fear. "To Alba?"

"No. To my friend. She has a farm."

Sergius's face screwed up as though he had to think hard about this. I began to wonder if there was something wrong with him. He'd been streetwise enough to find his way through Rome but had not enough wit to tell me all of his name or who this woman called Alba was until I'd pried it from him.

If Alba owned the boy and I stole him away, I'd be taken to court. If I returned him, he'd go back to being a body to fulfill some senator's lustful fantasy. One of those fantasies could get Sergius killed.

I prayed Mars was looking out for me today, and made my decision. I'd take the boy to Marcella, and if this Alba fussed about it, I'd ask Cassia to come up with the money somehow to pay her off.

"Never seen a farm," Sergius said doubtfully.

Cassia stood and went to him, leaning down to speak in a bright tone I'd never heard her use. "Well, today you will, my lad. I'll mend your cup, and Leonidas will bring it to you later." She straightened up, reached to him as though to pat his head, then withdrew her hand before it touched his greasy hair.

Marcella would bathe him. She had a spring on her farm, which she diverted to her own makeshift baths, and her children spent every summer day in them. She laughed and said they were half fish.

I held out my hand. Sergius, at last making up his mind, came and took it.

Cassia sent me a look I could not interpret. I ignored her and led Sergius out.

I saw Cassia dart back to her table to make a mark on her tablet as we left, likely the time I departed and where I was going. I felt relief more than annoyance. Her record-keeping had saved my life more than once.

❦

I TOOK SERGIUS THROUGH STREETS THAT HAD emptied for the heat of the afternoon. The sixth hour had passed—work was finished, time to sleep out of the sunshine or head for the baths to while away the bright hours of the day.

We walked toward the Forum Augusti. From there we'd make our way to the Porta Capena as Marcella lived a few miles west of the city along the Via Latina.

If Selenius's body had been discovered, there was no sign of it in the people who wandered around the end of the Forum Augusti's walls and down to the district called the Carinae. No one pointed at me and cried *murderer*! At least not today.

Even so, they noticed me. As they had this morning, people pointed, whispered, noted my passing. They'd wonder about the boy now too.

I halted at the corner of a lane that led to a small piazza. A narrow fountain spouted from the side of a tall tower that connected to the aqueducts, the over-flow from the fountain's stone basin sliding down the street until it found the nearest drain in the concrete curb. Most fountains did this, rendering Rome's streets damp streambeds. Water flowed constantly into and out of Rome without a break.

I crouched down next to Sergius. "Do you know a faster way to the Porta Capena?"

The lad nodded readily, as though he'd been waiting for me to ask.

I rose and took his hand, letting him pull me along through the packed houses and apartments between the Oppian and Palatine hills. If we continued on this road, we'd skirt the Palatine and turn near the Circus Maximus to reach the gate, a route that would take us through some of the most populated streets in Rome.

As I'd hoped, Sergius knew a way around. He moved unerringly down a side passage to a scarred door much like the one he'd brought me through earlier.

This door was locked, but Sergius lifted an iron sliver that had been tucked under a rock, picked it open, and returned the iron sliver to its place. No one paid any attention to him, I noted. They looked at *me*, but they took no heed of what the small boy a few feet from me was doing.

Sergius opened the door a few inches and slid through. If I hadn't been watching him, he'd have disappeared before I'd been aware. I waited until the street cleared a bit then caught the door before it closed and slipped inside after him.

I found myself in a dark, narrow passageway that smelled of urine and decay. For a moment, I imagined myself in the outbuildings of an amphitheater, waiting with both beasts and men to go to what might be our last fight. Darkness crept over my mind, wanting to suck me into it, but I shook it off and hurried after the boy, the sound of his footsteps guiding me.

The passageway led downward, and the floor grew wet as I descended. Soon my large sandaled feet sloshed in water and who knew what else, the walls now damp to my touch. I came to a branch in the passageway, emptiness to the right and to the left. I could no longer hear Sergius.

"Hey!" I shouted.

My words echoed back to me, but no reply from Sergius.

The darkness was complete, the light that had streamed through the cracks of the outer door far behind. I felt a rush of air to my left, and the soft grunt of a man striking out.

My instincts, honed from years of training for the deadliest games in the world, had me grabbing the wrist of the hand that came at me, turning it back and breaking the bone, even as a knife slashed through my tunic, biting into my flesh.

CHAPTER 4

THE MAN WAILED. I HEARD A THUMP AS HE FELL back against the wall, and another cry of pain. A knife clattered to the damp floor, and I picked it up. It had cut me, but only a glancing blow.

"Don't kill me," the man wheezed. "Please ..."

I groped until I found him then hauled him up by the back of his neck. He continued to plead and beg, and he smelled like filth.

"Who are you?" I demanded.

"No one." His whisper was hoarse. "No one."

"Tell me, *No One*, do you know the way from here to the Porta Campena?"

His groan cut off. "What?"

I squeezed his neck a bit harder. "Do you know where this tunnel leads?"

"Yes, yes. Don't hurt me anymore. Sir."

I wasn't a patrician or an equestrian and never would be, but I didn't correct his use of the honorific. Down here in the dark, I could be anyone.

"Show me," I said.

The man trembled all over. I loosened my grip but not enough to let him run away. He shuffled forward, me half supporting him with one hand on his neck, the other under his unhurt arm.

We moved a long way through the barrel vault of the tunnel, the stench of the damp floor nauseating.

I didn't usually mind closed-in spaces, feeling safest in my life when I'd been holed up in my tiny bedchamber in the ludus. The cell at the ludus had been my sanctuary, a place where no one expected me to do anything but lie on my back and wait for the next day. Perhaps that's why I slept so much now—bed was the only place in which I felt protected.

But this noisome corridor was not the same as my dry little room at the ludus where Xerxes had scratched erotic pictures onto the walls for me. It was wet and stank, and we kept going down, down into blacker darkness. I expected to find raw sewage at any moment, and the rush of water from under every latrine and domus in the city, carrying away leavings of its citizens. Romans considered gladiators excrement, but I had no wish to become it in truth.

The tunnel began to slope upward again, and at long last, I no longer waded through liquid. After the tunnel dried out, a slit of light cut through the wall and made me blink.

I'd learned how to keep flashes of light from blinding me—an opponent could move his shield to catch the sunlight and beam it into the small eyeholes of my helmet. If I let such a thing distract me, it would be for the last time.

The man I propelled along obviously hadn't had arena training. He screwed up his eyes and tripped, and would have fallen had not my firm grip kept him on his feet.

The chink of light belonged to a wooden door whose vertical slats had warped as they dried in the sun. The door was locked, but the latch that held it was easily broken with one shove. We emerged into a narrow street that looked like all other narrow streets in Rome. The smoke from a tavern mixed with the stench of slops and a waft of spice from a nearby warehouse.

"Where are we?" I asked.

The man peered about, barely able to open his eyes in the bright sunshine—he must have been in the tunnel a long time. "Bottom of the Caelian Hill," he said breathlessly. "Near the old wall."

The Caelian was a smaller hill across from the Palatine, the base of it filled with tiny lanes and too many houses. Finer houses spread out as the hill rose, and an aqueduct marched across the top, its arches raised against the sky.

I studied the man I held. He was grimy, his smell unfortunate, his face black with muck, his skin dark from both the sun and whatever were his origins. I'd thought he would be older, but a fairly young face turned up to me, his dark eyes above unshaven cheeks filled with pain. I'd cut his skin when I'd broken his wrist, and the blood had stained his tunic and the pathetic remains of his sandals. He might have been twenty at most, which was a man by Roman standards, but his look was that of a youth.

He was also a slave, I realized by the tattered remains of his garments. A runaway one probably. Not that I would immediately haul him back to his master —if the master had been good to him, he wouldn't have run.

He gaped as he took me in, finally seeing what sort of man had hold of him. "I didn't mean ... I didn't mean ..."

"To try to rob me in the dark?" I finished for him. "An easy mistake."

"I thought—" He broke off, his gaze going to the scar that ran down my neck. "Who *are* you?"

"You'll have to get that wrist seen to," I said, ignoring the question. "The best *medicus* for setting bones is Nonus Marcianus. He lives at the bottom of the Aventine, near the fountain of the three fish. Tell him Leonidas sent you and that he should go to Cassia for his payment. Can you remember that?"

The man stared at me in shock. "Leonidas?"

"Yes, *that* Leonidas," I said impatiently.

He shook his head in confusion. "Never heard of you. I meant that the name is unusual. Greek—Spartan. But you don't look Greek."

The fact that he didn't know of Leonidas the Gladiator surprised me. I had been the most famous fighting man in all of Rome until the last year, and everyone in Rome went to the games. I'd traveled with my lanista for exhibitions outside Rome many a time, so people the length of the empire had seen me. Either this man was from a very remote outpost, or he'd been living in the sewers a long, long time.

"Go to Marcianus," I said firmly. "Remember, fountain of the three fishes. Ask there for him."

The man nodded, his greasy hair falling into his
eyes. Nonus Marcianus would not thank me for
sending him this squalid specimen, but I knew he'd see
to him without hesitation.

As the man finally shuffled away, I heard light footsteps. Sergius came running down the street to me,
having popped through another door.

"I lost you!" he said breathlessly, panic in his voice.

I held out my hand, hiding my relief. "Now I am
found again."

The relief startled me. I had fully prepared to walk
through the tunnels in search of the boy if I had to, and
the thought of not finding him had made me cold.

I put my speculations about these feelings aside as I
led Sergius onward. Both of us were dirty and smelly
from the tunnels, but the people we passed as we
walked under the aqueduct and out through the gate
were just as stained from travel, tired and ready for
journey's end.

I wondered if any of the travelers had the slips of
papyrus they'd take to a shipping agent or money-
changer to redeem the equivalent of the funds they'd
paid into an account in their own cities. They'd be
unlucky if they'd been told to go to Selenius to collect.
If it was discovered the slips were forged, they would
be worth nothing.

It set me to thinking. Had a traveler approached
Selenius with a forged chit, and Selenius indignantly
refused to honor it? Had the man with the forged
paper grown enraged and murdered him?

Or was Selenius the forger? He could give the false slips to confederates who'd take them to the far corners of Rome, where agents might not realize the forgery and give out the coins. A nice scheme, if true. Selenius and his friends could divide the money without it costing them a single *as*.

Perhaps someone in the provinces had caught on to the fact that he was being robbed. That man might have come to Rome to confront Selenius, even to kill him.

I had little doubt that Cassia had already considered these speculations. While I traveled to the country, she'd be finding out who Selenius's confederates or angry customers might be. How Cassia would discover these things, I didn't entirely understand, but she knew every slave and every scribe in every house from the Palatine to the top of the Esquiline and every villa beyond that.

We weren't going far, but I tagged along behind a merchants' caravan, holding tight to Sergius's hand, carrying him when grew he tired. Even this close to Rome, even in these peaceful times, even in the middle of the afternoon, robbers could hide and strike a lone, exhausted traveler. I didn't worry for myself, but having to look after a child would hamper me if I had to fight.

The merchant didn't mind me joining them—he welcomed the muscle against robbers. Carrying Sergius must have made me look trustworthy, because the merchant didn't seem to worry about *me* trying to rob him.

I strode in silence, and Sergius offered no conversation. I realized as we went that I didn't know how to talk to children. I didn't much know how to talk to grown men either, so that wasn't such a surprise. But I hadn't given up the vague idea I'd have children of my own one day. It would be a quiet upbringing if I couldn't think of anything to say to them.

Sergius eventually settled into the crook of my arm and fell asleep against my shoulder. It puzzled me he was so trusting of me, if men at his brothel had used him as I suspected they had. But then I was Leonidas, the hero on his cup come to life. Perhaps he saw me as his champion, or maybe he was too simple to understand I could be as dangerous to him as any drunkard in a brothel.

Marcella's farm lay five miles outside the city. I left the Via Latina at a crossroads, saying farewell to the merchant and suggesting a safe house along the way to spend the night. We parted, and I made my way over a hill and into a green valley.

I'd always marveled that Xerxes had come out here most evenings to look after the farm and his wife, and then hastened back to the ludus the next morning for training. He'd been a slave, sold to the ludus by his former master when it was clear he'd do well as a fighter, but he'd been allowed to marry and move into Marcella's farm. Our lanista believed in giving us rope, but only so much. Xerxes wouldn't have gotten far if he'd tried to run.

But Xerxes had always returned, right on time for training—he was a stickler for duty and his honor. He'd died for that honor, leaving Marcella alone with five children to raise.

On the other hand, if Xerxes had tried to run away and been caught, he'd have been sent to the mines or quarries, which would also be death, only slower. At least in the amphitheater, he'd gone out a hero.

Marcella didn't see it that way. She'd loved Xerxes and deeply grieved his passing. Still did.

Her farmhouse was a square building presenting a blank face to the world, with its doors and few windows overlooking a protected courtyard. At night, she brought in the animals and her equally wild children, and locked the place tighter than the best fortress on a hostile border.

Marcella was in the courtyard with one of her daughters, a mite with long black hair and Xerxes's merry eyes. She and Marcella were milking a goat that wasn't happy with the process. Sergius, who'd woken, looked about with interest.

Marcella rose from the ground, her mouth open as she saw me walk into the courtyard. Her daughter caught the goat before it could dart away, holding it with her arms around its neck.

"Who in the name of all the gods is *this?*" Marcella planted her stare on Sergius.

I set the boy gently on his feet but he looked as skittish as the goat. "This is Sergius. I ... found him."

Marcella only raised her brows, waiting for an explanation.

I would never have called Marcella pretty—her dark hair was too thin, her body fleshy rather than curved, her face too flat. But she had a vitality that made a person forget she was plain. I'd met courtesans praised for their astonishing beauty who'd be invisible next to Marcella. I understood why Xerxes would have done anything for her.

There were five little Xerxes on this farm, three boys and two girls. Marcella ruled them with a firm but kind hand.

"And you decided to bring him to me?" Marcella demanded as she ran her dark gaze over the thin boy.

I shrugged. "Xerxes always told me he needed more hands in the fields."

Her lips firmed. "This lad couldn't lift a rake. He'll need a lot of feeding up before he's any use on a farm."

Sergius stared up at her, his mouth open, a mixture of fear and interest in his eyes. Marcella joined us and crouched down next to him. "I've just made a stew, child. Would you like some?"

Sergius glanced at me for confirmation, and when I nodded, he turned back to Marcella. "Yes."

"Oh, he can speak," Marcella said. "That's a mercy. Fabricia, turn her loose and take Sergius inside. If your brothers and sister remember to come in for dinner, we'll eat."

Small Fabricia unwrapped herself from the goat, who tottered two steps and then halted to graze on stray bits of grass. The little girl, who hadn't lost her smile since I'd walked in, waved at me and took Sergius by the hand. She towed him off, Sergius looking back at me uncertainly, but I saw his curiosity about not only his surroundings but Fabricia as well.

I held out one of the few coins I carried. "I'll send more money for him when I can. And visit him."

Marcella straightened up, pulled pieces of straw from her hair, and accepted the coin. She'd need it, and she knew it. "I suppose you'll tell me the story some-day. How is your other stray—I mean Cassia?"

Marcella had the idea that I let Cassia live with me out of kindness. I shrugged. "Cassia is Cassia."

"Good. I like her."

She studied me with her lively dark eyes, as though she expected me to say more about Cassia. I kept silent, not wanting to blurt out anything about murders and forgeries, not until I made sure I wouldn't be arrested for the crime. I didn't want my ill fortune coming back to haunt Marcella and her brood.

"You are well?" I asked Marcella when the silence had stretched to awkwardness.

For a moment, Marcella's animation deserted her, and I saw a blankness that I sensed many times in myself.

"Well in body," Marcella said. She put a hand on my wrist. "You are kind to ask."

Her touch meant nothing more than gratitude. I knew that. Marcella had only ever loved Xerxes, and he her.

I had no intention of offering bodily comfort to Marcella, if I could even perform on command, and she had no intention of accepting it. I'd once suggested she find another husband to help her, and she'd laughed at me, telling me she'd pushed out enough children, thank you very much.

Marcella withdrew her hand. "I might have enough stew to tempt even your appetite. If not, I'll round up something."

"No need. I'll eat when I reach home."

Marcella gave me a doubtful look. "It's growing late. You won't reach Rome before dark."

"I walk quickly," I said with a faint smile. "I don't want to leave Cassia alone."

Marcella regarded me without speaking for a moment. "I see. Greet her for me. And don't worry — I'll look after your boy. That is, if you promise to return and tell me how you found him, and why you decided you should be responsible for him."

I nodded solemnly. "I promise."

She burst out laughing, something Marcella could do spontaneously. I didn't always know what she found funny, but she had a comforting laugh.

"Go on with you, Leonidas. May the gods look favorably upon you."

"And you," I returned. We exchanged another look, she still finding something very amusing, and I went.

I HAD TAKEN A LONG TIME TO WALK FIVE MILES TO Marcella's, as the merchants had moved slowly to conserve the strength of their donkeys and their own feet. Traveling back took less time, as I moved at my own pace in the falling darkness.

It was dangerous to walk alone at night, even for a large and terrifying man like me. I'd easily take on any lone attacker, but a dozen men could have me on the ground before I positioned myself to fight. Bandits weren't known for following the rules of one-on-one combat. Gladiators fought plenty dirty, but we were nothing compared to desperate brigands.

I relied on the fact that I looked like a man who didn't have two coins on me to keep the robbers away. I wore a simple tunic belted at the waist and sandals, the dress of a freedman. No one would mistake me for anyone of high birth and fortune. In Rome, a man's clothing denoted what he was—slave, patrician, senator, a retired gladiator. The penalty for pretending to be in a different class could be dire.

I rarely had the chance to walk alone under the stars, and I found myself enjoying it. The air was cool, the sky open above me, the space of the gods filled with thousands of lights, some brighter than others.

As I drew closer to the city, the tombs of prominent Romans surrounded me, cold monuments to what once had been living, breathing people. I was tired of death, but these marble and concrete tombs did not bring me melancholy—they were monuments to honor memories, not bloody bodies strewn in my path as I walked from the amphitheatre, surviving once more.

I did not worry about gaining entrance to the city. Wagons and carts were only allowed in to make deliveries or take wares out again in the middle of the night. The edict made sense, as any other time of day, the heavy vehicles would block the streets, and we'd be bottled in.

Citizens paid for the convenience of moving about more easily during the day by nights filled with noise. Warehouses backed onto apartments, and a single domus might have storage houses all around it, with wares delivered after dark.

I was never bothered by the noise—I slept through it all—but it drove Cassia mad. She'd been raised on a villa in Campania where her father had been a slave, and where all had been, she said, blissful quietude.

One day, perhaps we'd have enough money to live in a small house in the hills—a modest home if not a grand villa. Of course, I'd have to find a way to buy Cassia or free her from our benefactor. She didn't belong to me; she'd been lent.

I caught up with another merchant a half mile from the gate, and earned a ride on the back of his cart filled with unknown metal objects in exchange for my protection. I dangled my feet from the back of the cart, whatever was in his bags poking me in the thighs.

We went through the gate without hindrance, and I slid off the cart near the Circus Maximus. The merchant headed for a warehouse on the Aventine, and I continued around the Circus and up to the Subura, after a farewell and a thanks. I still didn't know what was in the wagon—bowls, urns, statues of gods?

I walked up the stairs to our small apartment, and inside.

Cassia launched herself up from the table and at me, her dark eyes wide, worry in every line of her. I felt her slim arms around my body, her many-curled head land on my shoulder.

"Leonidas," she said brokenly, in a very un-Cassia-like way. "They found Selenius. The vigiles said they'd scour the city for you, and you didn't come home. I thought ... I thought ..."

To my astonishment, she burrowed her face into my tunic, trembling and holding on hard.

CHAPTER 5

"THEY CAN'T BE SEARCHING FOR ME VERY diligently." I rested my hand on Cassia's back, finding it supple and warm under her linen gown. "I walked from the Circus without seeing a one of them."

The vigiles were night watchmen whose main job was to keep public order and look for fires—if a fire broke out, they hastened to pull down houses to prevent the spread of flames. A mob of them might track down a killer, but if their commander thought they had better things to do, they'd let others find and drag the criminal to the magistrates.

"I traveled with a merchant and his family on the way," I went on, feeling the need to explain. "It took more time to reach Marcella's."

Cassia unwound herself from me, and I let my touch slide from her. She wiped the back of her hand across her eyes, which were red-rimmed and wet.

"Of course," she said. "I knew it would be something like that. Or that you'd decided to stay the night at the farm. You ought to have." Cassia took a step back. "Why didn't you? It was dark …"

I shrugged. Then yawned. I was exhausted and my bed beckoned. I should be as worried as Cassia that Selenius had been found and men were searching for me, but …

"Why are they looking for me?" I asked abruptly. "Was I accused?"

Cassia wiped her eyes again, tucking back a lock of hair that had tumbled down. "Not yet. But another shopkeeper near Selenius's stall said he saw you. Others observed you visit Quintus the baker before that, and Quintus volunteered that he'd sent you to Selenius to collect a debt. The shopkeeper in the *macellum* can't be sure when he last saw Selenius alive. Before you went in search of him, anyway."

I silently called down every curse I could think of on Quintus the baker and observant shopkeepers.

I should have felt more fear, anger, or indignation at the very least that I'd be taken in for killing a man I hadn't. I had been worried about just this thing earlier.

But after visiting Marcella, remembering Xerxes, I was numb—nothing penetrated the fog in my head.

I was tired, I told myself. Cassia had awakened me from sleep too abruptly this morning, and I'd spent the day running around tunnels in the city followed by walking the five miles to Marcella's farm and back.

I turned away from Cassia and sought my bedchamber, stumbling in my haze of fatigue.

Cassia stepped in front of me. "You can't go to sleep now—we must clear you of this murder."

I gently brushed past her. Cassia would have to

find a way to help me on her own, and I trusted that she would.

As I more or less fell onto the bed, I thought about the tunnels Sergius had showed me, and realized that anyone who knew of them could have crept undetected into Selenius's shop. The man who'd attacked me showed that desperate people might lurk in the tunnels, looking for a victim to rob.

I'd tell Cassia about them. Show them to her. She'd no doubt figure out exactly how much time it would take for a man to slip through the tunnels from every part of the city and out again in any other part, drawing little maps and diagrams to explain it to those who could not understand.

I was already half asleep by the time my reed bed crackled beneath my body. I heard Cassia let out a long sigh, then felt my sandals loosen and slide from my feet. A light blanket found its way across my legs, cutting the cool breeze that curled through the open window. Cassia hummed quietly, as she often did, but then the sound cut off.

"Oh, Leonidas," Cassia whispered. "Whatever will become of me if I lose you?"

A good question. She could not return to her former mistress, and our current benefactor might find a less salubrious man to lend her to, one who might beat her or force her.

I needed to stay alive, and free, to keep her safe. I would clear my name, and Cassia would help me.

It was my last thought before oblivion. Tonight, I hoped, I would be able to rest without dreams.

❀

THE DREAMS LEFT ME ALONE UNTIL DAWN, AND THEN
they came swooping.

In them, I saw Selenius, standing upright and
regarding me calmly while blood flooded from his
sliced throat. He didn't seem to be aware that he was
already dead—he only held out a slip of paper,
demanding a huge amount of money for it. I couldn't
pay, but he offered to take the boy Sergius in lieu.

I shouted at Sergius to run, but the lad was frozen
in place, staring at me in terror across the blood-
drenched floor.

It's all right, Marcella whispered from far away.
Sergius is safe. You took him to the farm, remember?

The voice changed from Marcella's to Cassia's, but
my worry only rose. Cassia should not be here. Selenius's smile when he saw her exactly matched the
shape of the cut in his neck.

I'll take Cassia instead, Selenius seemed to say. *Beautiful morsel. Proud bitch. Better on her hands and knees, I
think.*

Another man had said those very words to me at
one time. I'd nearly killed him. I lunged at Selenius,
and his blood showered me as he fell, warm and
stinking.

"Leonidas!" A blow fell on my stomach, a strangely
light one.

The thump didn't fit with my dream, and I swam
toward light, blinking open my eyes to see Cassia
standing at arm's length, her stick tapping me just

above my navel. The blanket was around my hips, tangling my legs.

"Leonidas," Cassia repeated, sounding relieved. "Marcianus is here."

❀

MORNING HAD BROKEN SOMETIME WHEN I'D BEEN asleep. Rome was washed with golden light, the cool of the night lingering in the streets to temporarily drive out the acrid scents of smoke, food, and humanity.

A man sat at our table, hunched in conversation with Cassia. He had a fringe of graying hair, a thin but well-muscled body, a bulbous nose, and brown eyes that in turn could be kind or stern. Kind when he was feeding me a tincture and telling me that setting my bone would hurt but he'd be swift, stern when admonishing me to rest and on no account fight for at least forty days.

His name was Nonus Marcianus, and he was a physician, a *medicus*, for Rome's most lucrative ludus. He'd been healing beaten-down gladiators for years, becoming an authority on broken bones, lacerations, wounds deep and shallow, and the chances a man had of living or not. His balms and potions, which he'd learned to mix in the East, had lowered the incidences of festering wounds and rotting limbs in our school. The gladiators, even the most brutish of them, had only good words for Nonus Marcianus.

He was a learned man of a Roman equestrian family, though born in the Greek isles, migrating to Rome after he trained as a physician in Greece. He'd taken to Cassia right away, as though pleased he'd found an equal in understanding.

They spoke Greek, Cassia relaxed and smiling as she chatted with him, Marcianus looking content as he answered her questions—or whatever he was saying. I couldn't understand a word.

Both broke off as I entered, and Marcianus rose. He wore a tunic that hung below his knees, and he'd laid his toga, the garment of a respectable citizen, across the back of his chair.

"Greetings of the gods to you, Leonidas."

"And you," I answered, trying to clear the sleep from my head.

I'd put on a clean tunic without Cassia saying a word. I'd had enough of the stained one I'd worn all day yesterday, which had been further ripened by my walk to the farm and back. I'd be visiting the baths today—the smell of unwashed gladiator was not my favorite.

"Your lanista rues the day he lost you," Marcianus said as we both sat down.

Cassia brought Marcianus a cup of wine, apologizing that it wasn't the best. Marcianus politely accepted. A bowl of nuts had found its way to the table as well. We never had much food in the apartment, but Cassia always managed to find refreshments for special guests.

"Does he?" I asked without much interest. I took up a handful of almonds and popped them into my mouth, enjoying their smoky flavor. Cassia bought them roasted with a touch of salt.

"Aemilianus has taken a contract with a patrician

putting on games in Ostia, I hear. The prices Aemil can ask have gone a long way down without you at the school. He toys with asking you to return to perform in special bouts."

I was already shaking my head. No more games, no more amphitheatres. It wasn't fear that kept me from fighting—I continued to practice and train, even dropping in for sessions with Aemil on occasion, but I refused to take another life. Ever. For any reason.

"I told him you wouldn't," Marcianus said, looking satisfied. "I will convey your answer."

I said nothing, only scooped up another handful of almonds.

Cassia seated herself at the table again, opening her tablet and taking up a stylus. She made a note—I wondered if she'd marked down the exact day and time I'd turned down my old trainer's offer to return and make him some money.

I knew why Marcianus had come. I'd told the man in the tunnels to seek him, and that Cassia would pay the fee, if we had any money to give Marcianus, that is. What I did not know was why Marcianus wanted to speak to *me*. He hadn't come to convey the message that my lanista wanted me to fight for him again—he wouldn't have bothered to trudge all the way across Rome for that.

"Who was the man you sent to me?' Marcianus asked. "It was a straightforward fracture—you twisted his wrist to block a knife thrust. Why did he try to kill you?"

Cassia's eyes widened, and she sucked in a breath. I'd fallen asleep before I could tell her about the man with the knife, and obviously this was the first Marcianus had mentioned it. "He attacked me in the tunnels," I said. "They are part of the sewers, I think. It was very dark, and he must have been hungry."

"Hungry and terrified," Marcianus said. "I set his wrist and gave him something to eat. He wouldn't say his name, and he ran off as soon as I let him go. But he was impressed with you."

I shrugged. "I hurt him pretty badly. I didn't want him to die."

Marcianus acknowledged this. "The wound didn't bleed much. As I say, it was clean. Very professional."

I shrugged again. I didn't admit how much the blood on the man's tunic, put there by me, had unnerved me.

Marcianus gave me a keen eye, as though he knew what was going on in my head. "I heard the vigiles were looking for you last night. They must have given up."

"They sleep during the day," Cassia said sourly. "I have no doubt they or the urban cohorts will try again later."

"I didn't kill Selenius." I spoke in a firm voice. I didn't think Marcianus would be sitting here so calmly if he thought I'd murdered a man, but I wanted to make certain he knew the truth. "I don't know who did."

"Tell me about his body," Marcianus said, interested. "I'll look at it if I can — who is his family?"

"I only heard of him yesterday," I began with a growl, but Cassia pulled another wax tablet to her and opened it.

"Gaius Selenius was unmarried," she said as she consulted her notes. "His house is on the Esquiline, where he lived with his sister, Selenia, and his nephew, who is also called Gaius Selenius—he adopted this nephew. The sister collected Selenius for burial, so I imagine his body is still at the house. Selenia and her son will inherit the business. I believe young Gaius is already having the shop cleaned."

Marcianus snorted. "He wastes no time."

Cassia did not look as disapproving. "Selenius's rivals will waste no time taking his customers. If the Selenia and Gaius need the business to live, they will have to make sure they don't lose too many punters to the taint of Selenius getting murdered in his own shop. You know how superstitious Romans are."

Marcianus's smooth face split into a smile. "So are Greeks, dear lady. But in a different way, I grant you. The sister and nephew will have to appease Selenius's spirit, yes, and any other spirits who took the opportunity of the violent death to flock in. And you are right. Such a thing should not be delayed. However ..." Marcianus returned his attention to me. "If I cannot convince the poor woman to let me have a look at her brother's body, we have only you, Leonidas, who can tell me of him. So please describe what you saw. Leave nothing out."

I didn't want to revisit the room awash with blood, even in my mind, but did want to hear what Marcianus made of the death.

I closed my eyes.

If I concentrated on a thing I could remember it in its entirety. I don't know whether this came from my training to always know where an enemy stood, or simply something in my humors, but I could picture a scene vividly for some time if I tried. Probably why I had so many nightmares. A curse from the gods, I thought it. Maybe one day I'd assuage whatever god I'd offended and be granted the blissful ability to forget.

"Selenius's shop," I said. "Ten feet on a side, and in height. Light came through the open wall above his counter, from the atrium in the center of the *macellum*. He was lying under the counter, head bent against the wall, feet spread. His right sandal had one thong broken. His tunic must have been recently laundered, or it would not have been so white. That made the blood on it so much more vivid."

I broke off, bile rising. If I hadn't been so worried about Sergius as I'd stood at the edge of the pool of blood, I'd have been out in a back lane, vomiting until there was nothing left.

Marcianus's tone gentled. "Can you describe the patterns the blood made? Think of it as paint—where had it been stroked?"

I swallowed. Paint and blood might look similar, but paint smelled clean in comparison.

"A line around his neck," I said. "A stream down his throat, though some had dried and was caked. His tunic soaked with it, like it had caught a wave from the sea." I swallowed again. "It spread from under his body, past his feet, to collect in a pool. It lapped almost all the way to the walls to either side of him. Only a small patch was left bare." I'd used that patch to step around the room to Sergius.

"Hmm." I heard Marcianus's interest but didn't open my eyes. "What else?"

I didn't want to mention Sergius. I trusted Marcianus with my life, but he was a conscientious man. If he decided Sergius had killed Selenius, or at least had witnessed the death, he'd hunt the child down and take him to a magistrate.

I wiped Sergius from the picture in my head. "There was a door on the other side of the room. I thought it led to the shop next to Selenius's, but it didn't. It went to tunnels that came out on a street not far from the fountain of Orpheus."

"Hmm," Marcianus said again.

"Hmm, what?" Cassia asked. "Your *hmms* have me most intrigued."

"It was a warm day," Marcianus said. "And yet you say the cut on his neck was black, the blood there dried. I can't be certain until I see this man myself, but I would guess he died somewhere in the fourth hour. Possibly close to the fifth, but no later."

Cassia gave a little victory hop in her chair. "Ha! Leonidas was asleep—sleeping quite soundly—until nearly the fifth hour yesterday. It took me the longest time to wake him. He left at a few minutes past the fifth hour—I made a note of it." She pulled out a tablet filled with scratches to show Marcianus.

Marcianus had seen Cassia's records before, but he still looked awed upon viewing them. By habit, every day, Cassia noted every single time I came and went from the house, and every time she did, every place we walked, every coin we spent, and on what. She claimed she did this to keep us from running out of money, but

I suspected she simply enjoyed it. A person can make a note of an expense without writing a lengthy record of every moment of the day.

"If your notes can convince a magistrate, then Leonidas has nothing to worry about," Marcianus concluded. "A witness to Leonidas's sleep or Selenius's death would be better though." He meant a witness to my sleep other than Cassia. A slave's testimony was not always regarded as relevant.

"Our neighbors," Cassia said in perfect seriousness. "They likely heard Leonidas snoring."

Marcianus chuckled. "You will have to ask, my dear. Leonidas, let me see your hands."

I frowned a bewildered moment, and then held them out, palm-up. Salt from the almonds sparkled on my skin. I hadn't had time to bathe, so I carried the dirt from walking through the tunnels, my journey to Marcella's farm, my ride on the merchants' wagon, and whatever I'd touched between the Porta Capena and home last night.

Marcianus clasped my wrists and dragged my hands to him, bending close to examine them.

His strength always surprised me. Marcianus was a small man, but he could yank a reluctant gladiator around with ease. I didn't like others touching me — I'd been pushed, shoved, and manhandled since I was a boy — but I'd learned to put up with Marcianus.

He leaned over my right palm until his nose nearly touched it, and then ran a fingernail over the crease between my forefinger and wrist. "No blood there. Even if you wash carefully, blood can linger in the tiniest grooves in the skin. If you'd killed Selenius, you'd have had it all over you."

Marcianus released me with satisfaction. He rose with his usual vigor, lifted his bunched toga, and looped it around his arms. He'd need more help to position it correctly, but Cassia remained seated. Draping togas, she'd told me, was no more one of her talents than dressing hair.

Marcianus drained his cup of wine, dabbed his mouth with the back of his hand, and headed for the door.

"I will visit the man's sister and try to examine the body," he said, pausing on the threshold. "Don't worry, lad. I'll make sure you aren't taken for it."

I'd stood up to see him out, though Marcianus was already halfway down the stairs before I reached the door. He waved up at me, turned the corner of the landing, and was gone.

Cassia remained on her stool. She studied her tablet, her smiles gone, her expression troubled.

I sat down on the stool Marcianus had vacated. "What?"

Cassia let out a sigh. "Nonus Marcianus will do his best, but the only thing that will clear you for certain, Leonidas, is finding out who truly did this."

I agreed with her, but there was no use restating it. "Why didn't you mention the forged vouchers?" I asked. When she hadn't, I didn't bring them up either, because I knew she'd have a reason why not.

"They may have nothing to do with the murder, and Marcianus might have asked why I hadn't alerted a magistrate about them right away. He is a stickler for the rules."

I reached into the bowl of almonds and closed my large hand around its remaining contents. "So are you."

Cassia gave me a prim look. "Only when it's expedient. Ah, well, I suppose we'd better make a start."

I dumped the handful almonds into my mouth and chewed. "You make a start," I said. "I'm for the baths."

CHAPTER 6

I HEARD CASSIA'S LIGHT STEPS BEHIND ME AS I walked out the door.

"Why on earth are you going to the baths when you're a wanted man?" she asked, quieting her voice so the patrons of the wine shop wouldn't hear. "You'll be dragged to prison."

I looked back at her. Cassia's dark eyes held fear, a lock of her hair escaping to brush her cheek.

"No one has come to fetch me is because they know I won't run," I said. "If I'm arrested at the baths, at least I'll be clean."

I turned away before she could argue. Strangely, she did not. When her voice came to me as I reached the landing, it was hushed.

"I'll prove it wasn't you, Leonidas," she said. "Marcianus and I will prove it."

I believed her. I'd never met a person with as much clarity of thought as Cassia. She'd explained, when I'd

remarked upon this once upon a time, that if I considered her intelligent, it was because her father had been
a brilliant teacher and writer, and he'd taught Cassia
how to think. *She* didn't believe herself to be unusually
clever — she thought she'd never live up to her father's
greatness.

No matter. I had faith in Cassia. She, a Greek
woman and a slave, had more honor and loyalty in her
than most Roman men who'd been raised to such
concepts. She'd not thank me for the comparison, but
it was true.

Instead of heading for the small bath complex I
usually frequented, I walked to the Campus Martius
and the Baths of Agrippa.

I preferred my friendly bathhouse near the old wall
under the shadow of an aqueduct, where slaves and
freedmen, along with plebs from the Aventine and the
lower slopes of every hill, mingled without inhibition.

The more ostentatious baths, like the ones built by
Agrippa seventy and more years ago, also welcomed
slaves and freedmen. But it was understood, if not
ruled, that we'd keep to ourselves and not interfere
with the enjoyment of our betters. The patricians and
equestrians also saw no reason not to order any slave
they saw to do their bidding, even if it was said slave's
afternoon off.

I sought the Baths of Agrippa today because large
bath complexes were founts of all gossip. If anyone
knew anything about Selenius and his murder, it would
be discussed in the *caldarium*.

I made for the Campus Martius via the Pallacinae

neighborhood and its lines of shops shaded by colon-
nades. I welcomed the coolness under the arches,
fading into the crush of shoppers and merchants on
this fine summer morning.

Rome would celebrate the festival of Fortuna soon,
and Cassia and I would join the festivities, which
would involve the death of unfortunate animals, a feast,
and plenty of wine. I'd eat a morsel of meat to honor
the gods, but I didn't have much taste for cooked flesh.
The wine I'd drink until I couldn't stand.

I skirted the enormous portico of the Saepta Julia,
which had seen gladiatorial games in its vast center. A
building crane rose somewhere behind it, men on a
high rooftop manipulating a stone block into place on
some new edifice, while the crane's great wheel slowly
turned.

I walked past the Pantheon of Agrippa, funded by
the man who'd dedicated many public buildings to the
honor of the great Augustus. Cassia told me Agrippa
was to have been Augustus's heir and the next princeps, but he'd died too soon. Perhaps the uncertainty
of these times could have been mitigated, she liked to
say, if he had lived.

I paid little attention to politics except to avoid the
intrigues that swept the city from time to time,
resulting in entire families dead or exiled. I preferred to
be a nobody not doing anything in particular, rather
than a patrician in a hilltop villa wondering when the
Praetorian Guard would come for *him*.

The bath complex I entered on the other side of the
Pantheon was grand. Columns soared to a lofty ceiling

held up by caryatids, paintings of lavish landscapes and villas covered the walls, and a mosaic of Neptune in his chariot pulled by sea serpents flowed across the main floor.

I stripped down in the *apodyterium*—the changing room—and found an eager attendant who helped me rub oil into every inch of my grimy skin. I even poured oil over my head, my hair kept shaved close enough that I could clean it that way. The attendant, who asked me incessant questions about what it had been like in the amphitheatres smacking my sword into my friends' guts, finally turned away to the next bather. I left for the gymnasium, which was under the open air.

I'd been to these baths only once before, but one of the trainers there, a former gladiator himself, long retired, welcomed me. He had wooden practice swords in a rack, and he and I hacked at posts set up at intervals around the room while the sun poured down on us.

The routine of the thrusts and steps returned to me, so familiar I could go through them while my mind floated.

The exercise shook off my fog. As it did, I realized something that others might not—a gladiator doesn't slice with his sword—he stabs. We'd been taught that a hard thrust was more effective than a swipe. I would have stuck my sword straight into Selenius's throat, not tried to cut him open.

The killer, I reasoned, must have come and gone through the tunnels. The shopkeeper and the two Gauls in the *macellum* had seen me enter, but they'd seen no one else, according to Cassia. That meant the murderer had either been a person they saw in the market every day and so didn't notice, or he'd come in and gone out through the tunnels, as I had. An avenue I would explore this afternoon, when the shops were quiet again.

The trainer admired my patterns and asked me to show him a few moves. We sparred in slow motion, attracting much attention from the other bath-goers. I kept my movements slow and deliberate, knowing that if my body felt the moves of true combat, I might instinctively go for the kill, no matter that our swords were carved from wood.

I ended the bout first, saying I needed to get on with my day. The trainer took my sword, slapped me on the shoulder and told me I could spar with him any time—he'd welcome the relief from tedium.

We parted. I fetched my strigil and had another attendant scrape the dirt and sweat I'd raised from my body, the oil taking it easily away.

I drew a crowd during this ritual. Each time the attendant flicked away the accumulated gunk, men would dive for it, scooping it in a cloth or small dish. The oiled sweat of a gladiator could be made into an unguent, which was believed to heal and give strength. The blood of a dying gladiator had even more potency, but I had no intention of giving them any of *that*.

I ended the entertainment by walking to the *tepidarium*, plunging into the pool to wash away what remained of the oil. Then I swam, stretching my limbs. I'd learned to swim as a boy fishing in the Tiber, far upstream of Rome. I remembered little of my childhood, but the cool rushing water under the

sunshine came back to me as I floated across
the pool.

I refreshed myself with a quick dunk in the cold
pool in the next room, then walked to the caldarium
and eased myself into the scalding hot water. Many
bathers choose to move from cold to tepid to hot, but I
preferred to go from freezing directly to heat.

My muscles softened and relaxed as I lolled on a
bench in the water. I leaned my head against the tiled
wall and let myself doze.

"Did you do it, Leonidas?" A man's voice drifted to
me. "Did you kill the money-changer?"

I opened my eyes. I first saw the reds, yellows, and
blues of the painted wall, a faux window opening to
green trees of a lavish garden.

Next I saw who'd spoken, a youngish man with his
short dark hair plastered to his head by the water, his
limbs slim but muscled.

I didn't know him, but in a city of a million inhabitants it wasn't surprising. His question meant word
had spread. The fact that I hadn't been dragged off to
the Tullianum to await trial and execution meant there
was doubt.

"No," I said.

He seemed to believe me. "But you were there. You
saw him."

"Yes."

The man was undaunted by my clipped answers. "I
heard about his sister. Such a pity." He shook his head
with the air of one confident such tragedies would
never happen to him.

"His sister?" I asked, trying to sound nonchalant. "What has happened to her?"

"It was long time ago. A few years anyway." He leaned closer to me, thrilled to be the one to impart the tale. "She was violated by another money-changer. This Selenius's friend."

He gave me a nod and withdrew, as though allowing me time to digest the information.

Poor woman. To be raped and then have her brother die violently was much to bear. I wondered if someone was out to gain vengeance on Selenius's family. Such things happened. I'd suggest to Cassia that we find out who'd attacked the sister—he might be the murderer.

"They say *you* did it," the man went on. He'd inched imperceptibly nearer to me. "So many saw you wandering about yesterday, but all say you had no blood on you at all. They also saw you with a boy. For enjoyment?" He wiggled his brows up and down.

"No." I snarled the word so fiercely the young man scooted down the bench again.

"Then what were you doing with a boy?"

Did he have nothing to do all day but chatter in the bath about other people? Probably not. If he was a patrician, he was probably an aedile, on the first rung of the ladder to senator. A pampered man's pampered son.

I realized I had to have some explanation for Sergius. I was a man people noticed, and they noticed what I did. "He was lost," I said, my voice retaining its growl. "I took him home."

"Ah." Disappointment coated the word. The young

man slid a little closer again. "My father imports the best wine. He gives me as much as I want for my own purposes. Share some with me?"

The hope in his eyes was unmistakable. There was no shame in a man lying in bed with another man as long as he did not do it to excess and kept his liaisons private. I preferred women, who were softer, smelled better, and were far less arrogant.

"No," I said abruptly and rose from the pool.

If I'd been any other freedman, the lad might have had his servants beat me for rudeness, but a hero of the games was given some latitude.

I stepped out, leaving him staring after me. Maybe the sight of my naked body would sate him for a while. I turned around briefly and let him see the rest of it — the least I could do for his information, whatever good it might do me.

He was wise enough not to pursue me, and I returned to the changing room, dried off and donned my clothes.

❦

IF NOTHING ELSE, BEING CLEAN MADE ME FEEL better. Now my stomach growled, reminding me I had missed several meals.

I left the Campus and its many entertainments and returned to the street of shops in the Pallacinae. I found a tavern and squeezed onto a stool at the corner of a table, asking the harried barmaid to bring me lentils and whatever vegetables they had cooking.

She returned before long with a bowl of lentils and

limp-looking greens, along with a crackling piece of bread. I dunked the bread into the broth and scooped up the lentils and veg, enjoying every mouthful, though the broth was weak and the vegetables old. The wine was indifferent as well, but I drank it down, thirsty after the hot bath.

I realized, when I was finished, that I had no money to pay. I'd given Marcella and the man who'd applied the strigil my last coins. Cassia hadn't known I was short of funds, or she'd have made certain I had at least the price of a meal.

I confessed my lack of coin to the barmaid. "My slave will be along later with it." Cassia would be vexed, but she believed in paying our debts as quickly as possible.

The barmaid, who had shining black hair and skin tanned from hot summers, cocked her head and assessed me. "No matter." She gestured for me to follow her. "Come with me."

I assumed she'd lead me to the back to wash up or stir pots of beans, but she took me up a flight of stairs to a tiny room dimly lit by a small square window. It had a slab of a bed covered with reeds, much the same as my own.

The barmaid began to undress. I remained in the doorway, not sure how to tell her she'd be disappointed.

I didn't have the chance. The barmaid caught my hand and dragged me to the bed, busily kissing me while she untied my belt and dragged off my tunic.

Then she proceeded to use me thoroughly. I don't think she noticed that this former gladiator couldn't raise his sword. She had me flat on my back, finding creative ways to take pleasure from me and my body. I'd been with women plenty—I'd been a fixture at a brothel near my ludus—but this woman, as much as she tried, delighted nothing in me.

I thought of Selenius's sister and her defilement. No doubt hers had been far more violent and terrifying, but I had an inkling of what she'd felt. She hadn't been a person to the man who'd taken her, only a body to be used.

But that was what a gladiator was, wasn't it? A fighting body, performing for money? It was why we were *infamis*, and why a barmaid thought I'd be more than happy to pay for my dinner by letting her play with me.

By the time she wore herself out and fell asleep, the afternoon had come, heating the city. I slipped away, sliding on my tunic and moving quietly down the stairs into the street.

I felt unclean, so I stepped into the baths close to home and washed my body all over again. It cost an *as* to enter this complex, but I told the attendants that Cassia would come by to pay later. They knew both of us and acquiesced. No paying my way with my body again today.

I was known and accepted in this bath complex, so I had to talk with men I'd become acquainted with while I soaked. That is, they talked, and I mostly nodded. But I learned why the vigiles had broken off their hunt for me last night and I hadn't been arrested by the cohorts this morning.

Apparently, the *garum* shopkeeper had reported

seeing a man come *out* of the *macellum,* but hadn't first seen him going in. The cohorts were now looking for this person, who had been described as dirty, young, and frightened. I had a feeling I knew who they were talking about.

The sky was darkening by the time I left the baths and made my way home. Cassia wasn't there when I arrived.

I stood in the doorway of our little apartment, looking over the room, my bed in the far corner, Cassia's little bunk on the other side of the table. A balcony opened to my right, larger than most as it was poised on the flat roof of the shop below.

I always knew when Cassia was out, and not because our domicile was so small I'd notice at once. I could walk in with my eyes closed and know she wasn't here.

The air was different, empty. Silent. Cassia was often humming or singing softly. Her two long stolae hanging on pegs near her bed and her cloak for cooler weather looked forlorn and waiting, as did her spare pair of sandals tucked neatly against the wall.

The table held her writing tools, tablets and stylus, papyrus and charcoal sticks, lined up exactly even with one another. In the middle of the table was the cup Sergius had dropped, stuck together again, the cracks in the clay almost invisible.

I lifted the cup, examining the crude drawing, running my finger over the letters that meant my name. *Leonidas*. A name that hadn't been my own, but Leonidas was who I became.

When I heard her step behind me, a tightness in me

loosened. Cassia began speaking as soon as she saw me, her words flowing around me.

"Nonus Marcianus told me how to mix a paste that would mend it in a trice," she said, motioning to the cup in my hand. "I saw him this afternoon, as I wandered about on all my errands."

I heard her unwind the *palla* that kept her head covered from the sun and mitigated the offense to men who disapproved of a woman running about by herself. Slave women did not have the same restrictions that patrician and equestrian women did—a Roman lady should stay at home and not show herself, unless she traveled in a covered litter or sedan chair with attendants. Cassia's former mistress had insisted Cassia never leave the house unless she was muffled, to keep shame from the household, she'd said.

Cassia went on she set a basket on the table. "When you take it to Sergius, perhaps I could go with you? To see the hills again, breathe air that doesn't have the stench of Rome in it would be ..."

She stepped next to me and inhaled as though trying to find the clear air of Campania in the heart of this city.

The breath cut off. I looked down to see her staring at me, her expression changing from her usual animation to bewilderment. She delicately sniffed again, then turned away, color rising in her cheeks. She blinked rapidly, ducking her head so I would not see.

I realized that though I'd bathed again after the tavern, the scent of the barmaid and her zeal must linger. Cassia would know what it meant.

I opened my mouth to explain, but Cassia bent over

the table, her back to me, her chatter resuming. "I went to the tavern while I was out and found us dinner — lovely, fresh endives and some greens, and there's bread left over from this morning. What did you learn at the baths?"

CHAPTER 7

Cassia laid out our dinner, as she did every night—a meal prepared by the tavern at the end of our street and a flask of wine from the shop downstairs. She'd instructed the tavern keeper exactly how to make the food I was used to, and now he and his wife prepared the dishes and had them ready as a matter of course.

I watched while Cassia poured two cups of the wine from a small flask, sweetening it with honey. She talked all the while, even though she'd asked me what I'd found out, never letting me speak.

I sat down and chewed through a salad that had been flavored with lemon, almonds, and a drop of honey, and endives roasted with a little vinegar and salt. The barley had been cooked in a rich broth of vegetables—I suspected some leftover pork ended up in the vegetable broth as well, but I didn't fuss. The meal was fresh and good, a far cry from the one at the other tavern.

As I ate, Cassia told me about her afternoon.

"I saw Selenius's sister, Selenia," she said as she neatly sliced off a bit of endive. "She has much to do preparing for her brother's funeral and helping her son take over the shop. She is shattered, Selenia is, but young Gaius seems capable enough. He's nineteen and has been assisting his uncle for several years, and at least understands the business. Gaius knows all about the forgeries, by the way."

I took advantage of Cassia putting the endive into her mouth to break in. "You asked about the forgeries outright?"

Cassia swallowed and sipped her wine. "I hinted. Young Gaius crumpled at once. He was so ashamed, and begged me to say nothing. His uncle, you see, and another friend, had come up with the idea. Selenius would give out these chits to select friends for nothing, they would hie off to whatever city accepted them, and the shipping agents there would pay out. The friends would then return to Selenius, and they'd divide the lot."

I'd thought of something similar as I dozed in the baths.

"Wouldn't the agents in the other cities catch on after a while?" I asked. "When their money was never replenished?"

"Ah." Cassia smiled, her melancholy fleeing. "That is the beauty of it. Selenius would pay back *one* of them. Then a man would arrive with another false voucher for a smaller amount of money from the same shipping agent. Selenius would then use that money plus more from the take to pay the next agent. Then one of his friends would withdraw funds from *him*, bring it to Selenius, and he'd pay the next one in line. He had all the agents believing they'd been paid back, when in fact, he was floating the same money from one to the other to the other. Astonishing."

Cassia sat back, a little smile on her face. Any clever arrangement involving numbers pleased her. The fact that Selenius and his friends had committed blatant fraud and theft was beside the point.

"Even so." I lifted my bowl, poured the last drop of broth into my mouth, and set the bowl down with a thump. "Someone would catch on eventually. Maybe they did."

"And were so angry that they killed Selenius?" Cassia finished, nodding. "I think so too. I've asked young Gaius to give me a list of names of these shipping agents who've been skimmed. I promised I'd say nothing—his uncle is dead and can't answer for the crime anymore—and Gaius will find a way to pay back all the money without argument. I'll discover if any of these men were in Rome yesterday, and if so, we'll find them and see if they indeed killed Selenius in a rage. Rest assured, your name will be cleared, Leonidas."

She spoke with great confidence, but I knew better than to relax. If Romans decided they wanted justice, they'd have it, no matter who had to pay. They might think a champion gladiator being torn apart by wild beasts a fitting end to the problem.

I finished my meal in silence. Cassia chattered on, about Selenia, the sister, and her grief. Cassia had pretended to be a slave working for Marcianus to gain admittance to Selenius's house and ask questions—in fact, Marcianus had accompanied her, saying he'd been sent to look at Selenius's body.

"Marcianus confirmed that Selenius was killed midmorning yesterday, as he suspected, which ought to clear you. You were fast asleep."

True. The idea of bed appealed to me, so I rose and set down my wine cup.

"They're looking for a man," I announced. "I heard this in the baths. A shopkeeper said he saw a man come out of the center of the shops but not go in, much earlier than he saw me. I think they're talking about the man I met in the tunnels. He was afraid, and he had blood on him." I'd thought I'd caused the blood on his tunic, but Marcianus had said I'd given his wrist a clean break, so perhaps not. "I'll look for him in the morning."

I mumbled this last as I walked into my bedchamber and kicked off my sandals. My tunic followed them to the floor, and I pulled a blanket around my naked body before stretching out on my pallet and entering the land of Morpheus.

MY OBLIVION LASTED A FEW HOURS AND THEN I WAS awake again. This happened sometimes—either I slept for a night and half a day, or I woke in the small hours, slumber eluding me.

I pulled on my tunic Cassia had hung on its hook and slid on my sandals, which were now lined up in perfect parallel by the wall.

The rest of the apartment was as neat, the supper

things long gone, towels folded, Cassia's tablets and papers stacked at exact right angles to the table.

I expected to see Cassia in her bed, curled on her side. In sleep was the only time she allowed herself to be untidy, her limbs askew and her hair tumbling.

Her pallet was empty, however, the blanket smooth. I felt a moment of alarm, then I heard a rustle from the balcony. Releasing a breath, I stepped through the doorway to the flat space that served as our makeshift terrace.

Cassia sat on the one stool that we kept here, a folding tripod she'd found secondhand at a market stall. She leaned back against the wall of our apartment, moonlight glittering on her tear-streaked cheeks.

I paused in perplexity. Cassia scolding, lecturing, teasing, or rolling her eyes at me I understood. Cassia crying, I did not.

She hadn't even wept when she'd discovered she'd been tossed from the lavish villa in which she'd grown up to be slave to a former gladiator, a brute of a man who was the lowest of the low.

My foot crunched on grit as I stepped out to the balcony. Cassia jumped and wiped her eyes.

"Did I wake you?" she asked with an attempt at her usual brightness.

I dropped to sit on the edge and dangle my legs over the wall. We had no railing here, wooden or otherwise, but the space was wide. We didn't worry about thieves climbing up from the street to our apartment because we had nothing to steal.

"No," I answered. "What makes you cry?"

I heard her start, as though she'd expected I would not notice. "Nothing important."

Though I'd lived solely with men all my life, I'd known enough women to realize this was not a true answer. Women said, *It's nothing,* when it was the most serious thing on earth.

I also knew that cajoling her would do no good. If Cassia did not want to tell me a thing, she would keep it firmly to herself.

I faced the street, listening to the rumble of delivery wagons and the shouts of carters in the distance.

We sat in silence for a while. A cooling breeze drifted through the narrow street below, driving away the smells and stuffiness of the June night. I thought of Sergius resting his head trustingly on my shoulder as I carried him the long way to Marcella's farm.

"I like children," I said.

Cassia drew an abrupt breath. "Pardon?"

"I like children," I repeated without turning to her. I mused on this for a moment. "I didn't know."

I heard a rustling and then Cassia was beside me, folding herself to sit and hang her legs next to mine. She stared off into the street as I did. "I think I do too," she said. "Or perhaps I simply like Sergius."

"Maybe."

Again we fell silent, both of us marveling at this new thing we'd discovered about ourselves. The coolness and moonlight transformed Rome into a silver and black mosaic, the harsh lines of the buildings softening, the smell of so many people packed together eased.

"Do you think our benefactor is keeping you from

being questioned for the killing?" Cassia asked in a quiet voice.

Our benefactor hadn't showed his hand, or the rest of him, for that matter, in our lives since he'd found me this apartment and sent Cassia to me. As far as I knew, he'd forgotten about us.

"I don't know," I said.

We watched the moonlight for a while, cut by the smoke from the perpetual fires burning to heat the baths. Entire forests had been razed to keep Romans in warm bathwater.

"You are a good man, Leonidas," Cassia said. "I will find out who did this crime and clear you of its taint. I promise you."

I rested my hand over hers and gave it a brief squeeze.

We sat again for a while before she gently withdrew her hand and climbed to her feet. Without a word, I stood and let her lead me back into the house.

I went straight to bed, exhaustion coming over me once more. I removed my sandals and lay down in my tunic this time, pulling the blanket to my chin.

As I drifted off, I felt the blanket be adjusted, a light hand resting briefly on my forehead. Then her voice, softly singing, Cassia's liquid tones easing the noise of my thoughts. Sleep came like a friend this time, and I surrendered into its arms.

❦

DAWN LIGHT TAPPED AT MY EYELIDS. "LEONIDAS!"

The frenzied whisper mixed with the gray light

woke me. I raised my head to find Cassia at the end of my bed, dressed, her hair coiffed, her eyes round.

I'd thrown off my blanket in the night, so I sat up, the tunic bunched around my thighs, and rubbed a hand over my face. I gave a wordless grunt for answer.

"He's here," Cassia went on in the same whisper. "The man who attacked you in the tunnels. He's asking for your help. Prostrating himself for it, I should say. Do get up—*please.*"

CHAPTER 8

I SWUNG MY FEET TO THE FLOOR, THE INSIDE OF MY mouth tasting musty. Barefoot, sleep in my eyes, I trod to the outer room, Cassia behind me.

My man from the tunnels was facedown on the floor, a mass of dark skin, bones, rags, and hair. A bandage wrapped around his right wrist, the only clean piece of cloth on him. He lifted his head when he heard me come in, his dark eyes filled with terror.

"Help me," he pleaded. "They're after me."

"Who?" I asked, but I knew. The magistrates needed someone to answer for this crime, and when they couldn't pin it on me, they'd find the next person any witness had seen. Exactly why I'd spirited Sergius out of town.

"I did not kill this money-changer," he said. "I was in the tunnels to hide, not to murder."

"And to rob," I said. "You attacked me."

"I feared you'd come to drag me back."

"Back where?" I demanded.

"The quarries," Cassia said from behind me. "Look at his hands."

Slaves put into the quarries or mines around the empire didn't last long. They were worked from dawn to dusk and beyond, given little to eat and little time to sleep. When one died, he was replaced with another. As there had been so many prisoners taken in battle and captured in vanquished cities throughout Rome's history, the next body wasn't hard to find.

"I come from Espania," the young man went on. "My name is Balbus. My master sold me to the quarries when he brought me to Rome. I ran away. I hid in the tunnels. Now they think I killed the money-changer. I never did."

For a flicker of time, I wished I was back in the ludus. There, I'd never had to think—every hour of my existence was planned. I knew exactly what I had to do every moment of the day. Even when I was out on my own, I knew how long the job I'd been hired to do would take and what time I was expected to return.

Now I had to decide for myself what to do. I could not pass off the responsibility to another person, or shrug and ignore the world.

Too many possibilities presented themselves to me. If I helped Balbus escape, I might be arrested for the murder with him. Even our benefactor might not be able to help me then.

If I did *not* assist Balbus, he'd be rounded up by the cohorts or the vigiles and tried for a crime he might not have committed. They'd condemn him to the games to be torn apart by beasts or throw him right back into the quarry to be worked until he dropped dead.

On the other hand, if I gave up Balbus to the magistrates, the crime would be considered solved, and I'd be left in peace.

But a terrified, desperate, and innocent man would die. I could not be the one who condemned him.

Then again, if I helped a wanted criminal and was caught and executed with him—what would happen to Cassia?

The last question made me pause the longest. If I were taken and condemned, Cassia might suffer a similar fate. When a slave killed a man in a house, all the slaves there could be put to death as an example to others. Cassia's life was not her own. The best I could hope was that our benefactor would step in and give her to another master, one who wouldn't be cruel to her.

I cursed our benefactor under my breath. A wealthy and powerful man—we assumed—had taken charge of our lives for whatever reason—and we didn't know who he was. When he could be useful and solve this problem, he was a ghost.

"Did anyone see you come here?" I asked Balbus.

"It was dark," he answered, his voice weak. "I don't think so."

I couldn't send him to Marcella. The thought of Xerxes's wife and children, along with Sergius, rounded up and sold into slavery for harboring a fugitive and an escaped slave rippled bile through my stomach.

"I know a place you can hide," I heard myself say.

Cassia remained silent. She not expressing an opinion surprised me, and I glanced at her to see that her expression held relief and approval. In her eyes, I'd made the right choice.

"Stand up," I told Balbus. My voice took on the tones of my toughest trainer. "You're going to be scrubbed and shaved. Then I'll take you to a place. You say nothing from now on. Understand?"

Balbus opened his mouth to answer, then closed it and gave a nod.

Cassia snatched up her palla and wrapped it around her, ducking past me and outside. She lifted the pot we used to fetch water as she went, and I knew she was on her way to the fountain at the end of the street. This would not be seen as unusual, as she moved purposely to and from this fountain every morning.

I had Balbus next to my bed, naked and shivering, by the time she returned, his rags of clothes in a corner ready to be taken out and burned.

Cassia kept her modest self on the balcony while I sluiced water over Balbus and scraped him down with my strigil—we had no oil, so water would have to do. I doused him again when I finished. The water was cold, and he let out a strangled shriek, which he suppressed when I glared at him.

I barbered him myself as well. I stropped a blade while Balbus watched nervously, and then I shaved him clean, face, scalp, and all. I was not trained with a razor, and usually had my whiskers scraped by the barber down the street, but I had a steady hand and only nicked him a few times.

I swept up his fallen hair and put it with his clothes to be incinerated—who knew what vermin was in it?

Any tunic I lent him would fall right off him, but

Cassia had already solved the problem. While I debated what to put on him, she came inside, averting her gaze, and thrust a handful of cloth at me.

This turned out to be one of her under-tunics, hastily cut so it would end just above Balbus's knobby knees. There wasn't much difference between a slave woman's garb and a man's, so I soon had him tucked into it, a rope tied around his waist.

Once I was done, Balbus looked a completely different person. Gone was the scraggly hair and beard that had hidden his face, and the dirt that had given him a foul odor. Before us stood a respectable-looking if overly thin slave, his broken wrist rewrapped in a clean bandage. I'd wrapped my own and my fellow gladiators' broken and sprained limbs often enough to become almost as good at it as Marcianus.

Only when I was ready to march the man out did Cassia come to me. "Where is this safe place you will take him?"

I shook my head. "If I don't tell you, you won't have to lie if you're questioned."

Cassia pursed her lips as she thought about this, and then stepped back and let us go.

I put a heavy hand on Balbus's shoulder and steered him out of the apartment and down the stairs. When we reached the street I ordered him to walk one step behind me, and if he valued his life, not to run off. I'd kill him myself if he did, I promised him.

It was the first hour, and Rome was coming alive. Plebeian men and women, freedmen, freedwomen, and slaves rushed about to buy food and drink for the day, and to run errands before the sun climbed too high.

Bakers shoveled bread into and out of roaring ovens; fish sellers yelled that their catches were fresh from the coast; fowl clucked and fussed; and vegetable sellers set out mountains of lettuces, cabbages, fresh green stalks of asparagus, and baskets of berries gathered from the nearby fields.

I could not resist pausing to buy a small measure of strawberries, using the coins Cassia had replenished in my pouch. I ate the bright, cool berries as we walked along, sharing a grudging few with Balbus, as a master might do with a slave.

Balbus was starving, I could see that. Where he was going they'd at least give him a meal. Probably a good one.

I took him to the river via the Campus Martius, not wanting to cut through the Forum Romanum at its busiest hour. We crossed the river at the Pons Agrippae and entered the Transtiberim, that growing expanse of Rome on the other side of the Tiber.

When the bored guard at my hiding place saw me, he gave a look of surprise, but unlatched the gate and let us in without question.

The sound of the gate closing after us gave me a moment's qualm, the habitual shiver at being locked in. I forced the qualm to pass, reminding myself that I could walk out again whenever I liked, a free man.

The yard behind the wall was full of activity. The morning coolness was as good for training as it was for the rest of Rome to conduct business and shop.

Men in nothing but loincloths industriously hacked at posts with wooden swords. Others built muscles by lifting lead weights or did various exercises under the tongue-lashing of a trainer, and still others sparred in the middle of the dirt yard.

Balbus looked around and shrank back. "This is ..." he whispered, then remembered his vow not to speak.

"My ludus," I finished. "This is where you will hide."

"LEONIDAS!" A GOOD-NATURED BELLOW FILLED THE yard, causing all training to stop.

The gladiators wiped brows, lifted off leather helmets, looked around. They stared—some in welcome, others in hostility, the *tiros* I didn't know in eager curiosity. A retired *primus palus* visiting the school was something to talk about.

The man who'd shouted had a body full of scars, a left ear half gone, and was missing several fingers on one hand. He was one of the hardest, toughest men I'd met in my life. Under his bullying, I'd become a champion.

At the moment, the man's grin could light the sky. "I knew you'd come back to me!" he shouted.

His voice was thunderous. All of Rome would know I'd come back too.

Aemilianus, or Aemil as he was called, had in his day been the most dangerous gladiator in the empire. He'd always fought to win, no draws. He'd retired ten years ago, bought a handful of gladiators and opened this school. He trained the best, like me and Xerxes, and aediles paid whatever Aemil asked in order to put on the most lavish games.

Aemil had the light brown hair of a Gaul, but what set him apart from other Gauls was that one of his eyes was blue, the other a green-brown color. He'd often fought without a helmet so that his mismatched eyes could unnerve his opponents, which was why he was missing part of an ear.

He had a Gaul's build, large and bulky as opposed to the shorter trimness of a Roman. Aemil had a theory that I was part Gaul too, as I was fairly tall and broad, and that could be true. I had no knowledge of my family. I'd been on the streets alone since my memories began.

"Who's this?" Aemil asked, staring bluntly at Balbus.

I grabbed the young man by the neck, which seemed to be the best way to haul him about, and drew him forward. "Can you put him to work?" When Aemil hesitated, I added. "I'll pay."

"You bring me a slave, and you'll pay *me*?" Aemil eyed Balbus, who had the sense to keep his mouth shut. "What's wrong with him?"

"Underfoot." I snapped out the word.

"Ah." Aemil nodded sagely. "Your woman doesn't like him. I can always use more help, so yes, leave him. What's his name?"

I shrugged. "Give him one." Aemil had helped me come up with mine, erasing whatever boy I'd been forever. He could erase Balbus too.

"Fine." Aemil turned to Balbus. "We'll call you Hermes, because you'll be fetching and carrying and being a messenger to anyone I say. You're too skinny for heavier work." He looked Balbus up and down again. "Slave to gladiators is the lowest thing you can become. Even lower than *me*." He chortled. "You going to live with that and not try to throw yourself into the river? I'm not feeding you and keeping you if you're going to wallow in despair. Understand?"

Balbus swallowed hard and nodded.

Aemil peered at the bandage on his wrist. "You wrapped that," he said to me.

"I broke it," I answered, offhand. "He irritated me."

Aemil shook his head then flashed me a grin. "So now I have to wait for him to heal before I can use him. No wonder you're offering to pay me." He turned back to Balbus and jabbed his thumb at the barracks. "Go in there and help clean it up. Then come and ask for work. I have plenty."

Balbus flashed me a grateful glance. I remained stoic, as though only ridding myself of an annoying slave, but I silently wished him luck. Emptying the slop buckets of gladiators was far better than being bound to a stake while a lion tore out his entrails, and he knew it.

Aemil watched the man scamper away before he turned to me. I held out my money pouch, but Aemil waved a hand. "Pay me by coming back, Leonidas. Go a few rounds with my new *primus palus* in the next games. The man's an arrogant turd, but good, very good. Not as good as you were though. Teach him some humility and make me money. What do you say?"

I thought of my old life—the days, weeks, months, years of monotonous training followed by the white-

hot desperation of a battle for my life. I hadn't felt fear
in the amphitheatres, only heat, determination, and the
need to survive.

The smell of blood, dead animals, and dead men
came to me, along with the odor of packed bodies in
the seats above me, the memory of sand burning under
my bare feet, the airless weight of the helmet locked
around my head, and the grim resolve in the eyes of the
man I faced, usually a friend I'd sat next to at the feast
the night before.

Aemil had shoved me into every game, sometimes
several rounds on the same day, taking more and more
money for my appearances, while he coolly negotiated
what compensation he'd receive if I were killed.

Aemil called himself the paterfamilias of our gladiator family, but he was a father who sold his sons to the
highest bidder. He was a businessman first and fore-
most. If I died spectacularly at one of these exhibitions
he wanted me to do now, he'd earn an enormous sum.

I took his hand and slapped the pouch into it. "I
say no."

Aemil's wrong-colored eyes flickered with rage, but
I cared nothing for his disappointment. I turned my
back on him and walked away.

I MADE MY WAY BACK OVER THE TIBER VIA THE PONS
Aemilius, its six piers stretching across the water just
south of the Insula. The Cloaca Maxima, the great
sewer, came through an opening in the thick embank-
ment wall not far downstream.

As I pushed through the flow of humanity on the bridge, the waste of the city pouring into the river not far away, my thoughts were scattered. Returning to the ludus always did that to me.

That part of my life was over, and I wanted it to be so, but what unnerved me was that Aemil's offer had been briefly tempting. I could slip back into the routine so easily, where I didn't have to think, but only do. They'd made me into a machine as mindless as the great mill wheels that ground the grain for our daily bread.

Whenever I entered the ludus these days, I had to fight to not take up a wooden sword and join in the training, and then file to the mess for my barley and fresh vegetables, and to my cell for a massage and to sleep. Over and over again.

I forced my feet to take me around the cattle market and through the valley between the Palatine and Capitoline, letting the stream of people, donkeys, and hand carts sweep me with them to the Forum Romanum. Columns of temples to both gods and government rose around me, towering edifices of stone that we surged, antlike, around.

I continued walking without ceasing, not halting when people called out to me, ignoring them to turn into the lane that led to the fountain where Cassia drew water, and thence home. My new home, where my decisions could affect the life of not only myself but the woman who'd come to depend on me, through no fault of her own.

Cassia was there. She'd heaped some bread on a plate and was setting it on the table when I walked in.

I snatched a hunk from the top and began to chew it as Cassia made a note of the time I'd returned. I trusted her notes did not mention Balbus at all.

"Shall you sit down?" she asked me from her stool as she tore off a miniscule piece of bread and bit into it.

"No," I said around my mouthful. "Going back out."

She frowned. "Where? You just got in."

I knew she'd persist if I didn't tell her where I was off to, so I said, "Selenius's shop. I want to ask the other shopkeepers about him. They must have seen *something*. Or someone."

Cassia nodded, her curls dancing. "An excellent idea. I'll come with you."

"No," I began.

"Do not worry, I will stand behind you like a good servant. I imagine the reason you don't want me to go is because your methods of questioning might be less than polite."

I couldn't argue, because she was right. I'd planned to be as brutal as people expected of me if necessary, which I should have done with the baker in the first place. If I'd shaken the sestertii out of Quintus and gone home, I wouldn't be in these current difficulties.

I finished my hunk of bread and washed it down with a cup of the wine merchant's cheapest vintage, while Cassia more carefully downed her piece. I needed to beat what the baker owed us out of him, or we'd be drinking piss and eating seeds fallen from the back of grain wagons before long.

"Come with me then," I growled, clattering my cup

to the table. "But don't talk. You drive a man to distraction when you talk."

Cassia sent me a smile of triumph. "Only because that man does not know how to answer." She fetched her palla and wrapped it around her body like a modest matron, and followed me out.

CHAPTER 9

WE WALKED THROUGH ROME AT ITS BUSIEST HOUR
to reach the *macellum*. Cassia kept a few steps behind
me, as a slave should, but the streets were so crammed,
we wouldn't have been able to travel side by side in
any case.

We had to step out of the way several times for
litters borne by Gauls, no doubt chosen for their huge
musculature. Inside the litter would be a matron or her
eldest daughter, perfumed and bejeweled, out to visit a
friend, or making a journey to a temple to petition a
god or goddess for whatever matrons and daughters
petitioned them for.

Lictors—men who accompanied patricians and
acted as bodyguards, messengers, and announcers—
pushed us aside at one point. The man they protected,
who was swathed in a toga with a narrow purple
stripe, swaggered by, chatting with another purple-
striped man, senators on their way to pretend to
govern Rome.

We had an emperor who'd decided he could do what he liked, when he liked, with whom he liked, and the senators could only discuss how to keep themselves and their interests safe from him. They were powerless, and Nero knew it.

That did not take the arrogance out of the men who walked by in their bubble of protection, or from the lictors who shoved us bodily out of the way. They carried bundles of staves, *fasces*, that symbolized the time when these highborn men could have their guards beat anyone they liked. The fact that the reeds were symbolic did not stop the lictors from using them for their original purpose if they felt peevish.

While I noticed the usual stares at me as I moved along, a half head to a head taller than most Roman men, we were not accosted. The streets were so crowded I doubted anyone could get close to me to arrest me for Selenius's murder if they wanted to, and if they did, they might cause a riot.

I led Cassia through the Subura, which was full of humanity—from the dregs who lived in miniscule apartments to wealthy men moving from their villas at the tops of the hills to the Forum Romanum, or to baths, temples, and everything in between. I could understand why Sergius preferred to travel via the tunnels that ran beneath the streets, as unsavory as they were. There, at least, it was quiet and not crowded.

We turned into the *macellum*, which was lively this morning. Vendors sold everything from produce and live chickens to cloth, carpets, lamps, beans, and cheap jewelry. Romans and travelers from all over the empire came to the market, many to use the money-changers who stood by their benches to switch the currency of far-off cities for Roman coin. On the fringes of the shops were cutpurses and thieves, waiting to relieve these foreigners of their gains.

Shopkeepers and their clients were too busy to gawp at a former gladiator striding in, his modest slave behind him with her basket. We moved without hindrance to the interior shops of the *macellum*, the sun shining brightly into its atrium.

Boards were in place over the counter of Selenius's shop, but I spied movement within the open door. I ducked inside, Cassia at my heels, to find a young man bent over a cupboard, a flickering oil lamp lighting the gloom. A male slave, middle-aged with a surly face and gnarled hands, swept the floor.

The young man looked irritably over his shoulder when he heard us enter, then he jerked upright and gaped at me.

Before I could speak, he saw Cassia. "Oh, it's you," he said, losing his worry. "The *medicus's* assistant." He must have assumed she belonged to Marcianus. "What do you want?" he asked as he returned to rifling the cupboard.

Cassia stepped in front of me. She kept her voice quiet and demure, her head bowed, showing the expected deference to the young man I gathered was Selenius's nephew and adopted son. She was good at playing her part.

"This is Leonidas, sir," she said. "He found your uncle."

Gaius Selenius the Younger jerked around again.

He had a jutting chin, short, flyaway hair, and small eyes. He looked much like the older Selenius, but with youthful vigor.

"Oh," Gaius said. "The gladiator." He concluded his assessment of me dubiously. "I've never seen you fight. I'm too busy to go to the games."

Most of Rome shut down during games, as they were public spectacles, often held in conjunction with religious celebrations, like Saturnalia. I wondered if his uncle or mother had kept him from going or if young Gaius was squeamish.

"What do you want?" he asked. "My mother is expecting me home. I am here to fetch my uncle's records."

"Leonidas offers his condolences," Cassia extemporized. "It is sad to lose one of the family. Your mother said you were very close?"

Gaius shrugged. "My mother loved him. He was her younger brother. I found him demanding and strict, but he raised me when my father died. He became a father in truth …"

The lad broke off, mouth twisting, eyes filling with tears. Cassia moved to stand next to him without touching him as she radiated sympathy.

Gaius cleared his throat. "I'm the head of the household now." The thought obviously terrified him. "My uncle shall have a grand funeral. And I will take over his business." More trepidation.

Cassia smiled encouragingly. "I am certain he would be honored."

Gaius didn't look so certain, but he accepted Cassia's polite concern.

The room had been cleaned of blood, though I could see where it had seeped into cracks in the floor. The wall where Selenius had lain had been scrubbed, the patch he'd leaned against now a bit whiter than the painted brick around it.

I studied the door to the tunnels. Cassia, catching my gaze, pointed at it.

"What is there?" she asked Gaius, as though curious.

Gaius glanced at the door but turned away, indifferent. "Don't know. Uncle never opened it."

"Maintenance tunnels to sewers," the slave with the broom volunteered. "Old part of Rome coming up to meet the new."

Gaius wrinkled his nose in distaste. "Have it sealed up."

The slave leaned on his broom, as though happy of the excuse to stop. "Costs. 'Swhy the master never did it."

"Yes, well," Gaius said impatiently. "We'll see the state of his finances, and if there's money, we'll seal it up. I don't want the smell coming in here."

"Deep part's too far down to bring bad air here," the slave went on.

Gaius scowled at him. He obviously wasn't having an easy time convincing his uncle's slaves he was in charge now. Some slaves were freed on their master's deaths, but not all, and some remained as freedmen doing the exact same jobs they had before, suffering the exact same blows when their masters grew irritated with them.

"Come," I said to Cassia, a slave who hadn't obeyed

me from the moment I'd met her. "My condolences," I said to Gaius. "May the gods bring you prosperity."

Gaius bobbed his head at my politeness, looking as though all the gods together with Fortuna leading the charge wouldn't do him much good.

Cassia gave Gaius a bow and meekly scurried to me as I turned to leave. She was the very picture of the demure, duteous slave. She would have made a fine actress, though she'd be offended if I told her so.

Once outside the shop and out of earshot of Gaius, she whispered, "We should look inside the tunnels."

I agreed, but there was nothing we could do while Gaius went through his uncle's things and the slave swept up.

We wandered through the shops instead, which were lit by the oculus above the atrium as well as arched openings high in the walls, and asked about Selenius and the day he'd died. That is, Cassia asked, and I frowned at the shopkeepers who tried to dismiss her outright.

No one had seen much of interest or out of the ordinary the morning of Selenius's death. Selenius had arrived at his normal hour, his nephew in tow. As per usual, young Gaius had left at midmorning to return home, as business was most brisk in the early morning. Several more customers had gone to Selenius and come out without being covered in blood or remarking on finding a dead body. A few described seeing Balbus go in—a hairy slave probably on an errand for his foreign master, they said—but they'd not observed him come out again. And they'd seen me.

They hadn't, to my relief, noticed Sergius. The boy

must have traveled back and forth through the tunnels, unnoticed.

The shopkeepers within the *macellum*, even the other money-changers, hadn't thought much of Selenius. He was successful, but less than honorable, happy when a customer didn't thoroughly count his takings.

Cassia, who was good at suggesting things until others opened up with what they knew, pried out from some of the other money-changers that they suspected Selenius of his forgeries, but they didn't know for certain whether he was guilty of them.

What they did know was that Selenius bullied his slaves and was firm with his nephew, though perhaps no harder on him than a master would be to an apprentice.

No one, it seemed, was very sorry Selenius was dead.

Cassia casually mentioned the network of tunnels that ran beneath the area, but none seemed to be aware of them. Rome was an ancient city—buildings fell to ruin and were rebuilt or burned, the ashes leveled and more built on top of it. I, like most Romans, was aware of the most important ancient monuments, like Romulus's hut and the rostra in the Forum, but the day-to-day buildings, even some of the most prominent temples, came and went. It was not so surprising that the shopkeepers didn't know much about the sewers that ran beneath us, only that they worked.

I found the *garum* vendor who'd noted my entrance to the *macellum* that day. The same two Gauls I'd seen lingering before were there again. Most Romans loved the fish sauce made by fermenting fish in salt — Cassia and I were exceptions.

The two slaves were quite tall and had very fair hair, which meant they'd come a long way from their northern homeland. Some of the prisoners brought back from the Claudian campaigns in Britannia had been very tall and pale, others small and dark. The larger ones made good gladiators — they were arrogant and ruthless fighters. The one who'd defeated Xerxes had definitely been merciless. He'd died under my sword in a later bout.

Cassia approached the *garum* seller's counter, producing a coin and asking for the fish sauce she hated. I imagined she'd throw it into the river the first chance she got.

The Gauls ceased their conversation and looked at me. We sized up one another, none of us speaking.

Cassia leaned to the shopkeeper, indicating the Gauls, who'd moved off, still eying me. "Is their master a regular customer?" she asked, as though curious about the odd foreigners.

The shopkeeper nodded, ready to gossip. "Sends them every day. He's fond of taking Gauls for servants. Has a house full of them. Blond giants, every single one of them, even the women." He chuckled.

"They were here the day Selenius was killed," Cassia stated.

The shopkeeper's amusement faded. "They were. I stay open later than most, as people often remember the *garum* at the last minute." He jerked his thumb at me. "I saw *him*. Going in."

"I saw *them* as well," I said, breaking my silence. "And you."

The shopkeeper finally understood that Cassia wasn't simply passing the time of day. He turned a sharp eye on me. "I never left this stall to go murdering Selenius," he snapped. "Anyway, why should I?"

I shrugged. "Why should *I*? I'd never met the man."

"Well." The shopkeeper waved a vague hand at me. "You're a trained killer."

"In a fair fight," I said. "What happened to Selenius was slaughter."

Returning my attention to the Gauls, I could imagine one holding down Selenius while the other cut his throat. They'd be strong enough to overpower him without much trouble, silencing him quickly.

But I'd not noticed any blood on them that day. They'd have been covered with it. However, they might have changed out of their blood-soaked clothes, bundling them into the large baskets they'd carried.

The two men regarded me without expression. I wondered if they were often blamed for whatever had gone wrong on any given day—when in doubt, accuse a slave. The shopkeeper, on the other hand, grew manifestly nervous. His worry might mean he was guilty, or only afraid he'd be accused and arrested, whether he'd committed the crime or not. Such things happened in our fair city.

He shoved the jar of *garum* at Cassia. "Take it and go. Don't come back here again."

Cassia calmly set the jar into her basket. "Cease

pointing the blame for this murder on others," she said. "And you won't see us."

She turned and stepped past the giant men who watched her without speaking. She walked by me too, as though she were a great lady and I her bodyguard.

I gave the Gauls and the shopkeeper one more stern look, and followed Cassia out.

❀

THE STREETS WERE QUIET AS WE EXITED THE marketplace, the sun reaching its zenith. We walked with a slower tread, the heat seeping into our bones. Even the beggars and stray dogs began to crawl off into the shade to sleep.

I wanted to start for home, but Cassia tugged my tunic. "Let's visit the baker first," she said. "You need to have another word with him."

She strode purposefully in the direction of Quintus's bakery, and I had to hurry to keep up with her.

CHAPTER 10

As he had been two days ago, Quintus was finishing his business for the day. He handed a round loaf of bread to a dark-skinned woman who loaded it into her basket and departed, giving me a startled glance as she walked away.

Quintus hadn't seen us, and he turned back to his ovens. "A moment ..." He shoveled several loaves out of one oven with his large bread peel and slid them into the tube-shaped holes in his wall to cool. "Now then, what do you—"

He froze when he saw me, his face becoming whiter than his flour-dusted tunic. "Leonidas." He upended the handle of the long bread peel and leaned heavily on it. "I swear to you, I do not have your money. That is why I sent you to Selenius. Now he's dead and can't pay me."

Cassia set her basket on the tiled counter, lifted out a tablet, and made a show of checking the marks within it. "You really ought not to employ the services of others if you cannot pay them, you know." She turned the tablet around and tapped a row of scratches. "Quintus Publius, ten sestertii."

Quintus paid no attention to Cassia or her tablet. He focused on me, his eyes filled with deep fear. "I have told you. Selenius owed me much. He cheated me. That's why I sent you to him. I thought if anyone could shake it out of him, it would be Leonidas the Gladiator …"

"Or, he was dead already," I cut in. "And you knew. You sent me to be caught for the murder."

I hadn't thought Quintus's face could lose more color, but his countenance became nearly as gray as the dead Selenius's. "I promise you I did not know. I did not know until the boy told me."

I stopped, my heart going cold. "What boy?"

Quintus waved his hands at the air over his counter. "Boy who hangs about the street. Don't know his name. Was following you that day. When I sent you off, he told me Selenius was dead and then ran away."

I carefully did not look at Cassia, who intently studied her basket. "You didn't call after me," I said to Quintus. "When the boy told you, you didn't try to stop me."

Quintus shrugged. "You were gone too fast. And I thought …" More lip wetting. "I thought that, if Selenius was truly dead —and I only had the boy's word for it, mind you —you'd at least search his shop and bring back the money."

"Then I would be in the Tullianum awaiting execution for stealing," I said. "I'm not a thief."

Quintus peered up at me as though realizing he had badly miscalculated my character. He didn't offend me — I'd given up that particular emotion a long time ago.

Cassia pushed her basket toward Quintus. "Will you put one of those loaves that are cooling in here, please?"

Quintus forced his attention to her, but shook his head. "They're promised to another. I have more inside —"

"No, one of those." Cassia pointed at the round openings that held the loaves he'd just taken from the oven. "You can make more for whatever wealthy man is buying them." She leaned across the counter to the Quintus, who was a head shorter than she was. "You owe Leonidas ten sestertii. He could take you to court for not paying him, and then you'd owe him more. Or he could bring suit against you for trying to make it look as though he'd killed Selenius." She straightened. "Or, you could simply give me a fresh loaf of bread."

Color at last returned to Quintus's cheeks, red blotches of it. He snarled, yanked one of the new loaves from its cooling place, and dropped it into Cassia's basket.

"Excellent," Cassia said. "I'll be back tomorrow for another."

"Another?" Quintus asked, startled.

"The price of a loaf is half a sestertius," Cassia answered serenely. "I will come to your stall for the next nineteen days, and you will give me a fresh loaf of bread made from your finest flour. Then you will have paid the debt." She lifted the basket and covered the bread with the cloth within. "Good day."

An emotion at last broke its way through my numbness as we turned away and left Quintus spluttering. It was mirth.

❦

THAT AFTERNOON, WE DINED ON FRESH BREAD, OIL, fruit, and boiled lentils. We sat on stools at our table, the door to the balcony propped open to allow in whatever breeze might amble down the lane.

We were somber as we ate, however.

"You don't think that little boy killed Selenius, do you?" Cassia asked me after a long silence.

Though I did not want to consider the question, I knew I had to. "It is possible," I said, turning over my thoughts. "When Sergius heard Quintus tell me to go to Selenius, the lad knew Selenius was dead. That means he'd seen Selenius's body."

Sergius had stared at me in shock when I'd arrived in the doorway—I'd thought because of Selenius's dead body. But perhaps he'd been running there ahead of me to cut me off, to try to keep me away, gaping in dismay when I'd found Selenius anyway.

Cassia gave me a morose nod. "Seen Selenius dead only because he plays in the tunnels? Or because he killed the man himself?"

"Why would he?" I tore off a piece of the bread, dunked it in my lentil broth, and stuffed it into my mouth. I chewed, spat the grit that lingered in every loaf into my hand, and swallowed.

"Perhaps Selenius tried to beat him," Cassia said quietly. "Suppose Selenius caught the boy sneaking around the tunnels, dragged him out, and beat him. The other men we spoke to said Selenius could be a brute. His nephew said so as well. Or—Sergius was a brothel boy, and Selenius might have grabbed him for another reason. Sergius could have fought back, grabbed a weapon—knife, even a sharp tile—and struck out." She touched her throat.

I shook my head, searching for any explanation to show Sergius could not possibly have done it. "The blow held strength. And landed in the exact place that would kill Selenius."

"He might have simply swung his weapon, and Fortuna did the rest. Even a small person can harm another when they are desperate enough." Cassia spoke from experience, one she did not like to talk about.

I drank a sip of wine. The vessel I held was copper, dented on one side of the lip, the bottom greenish from corrosion. "I don't want it to have been Sergius," I said in a firm tone.

Cassia gave me an understanding look. "What will you do if...?"

"Nothing." I set down my cup. "The hairy slave who was seen leaving the shops has vanished. Selenius's sister and nephew will have no one to prosecute. They'll hunt through the countryside for the slave for a while, but then give up."

Cassia nodded. "And the matter will die." She let out a long breath. "You know that even if Sergius or Balbus did not kill Selenius, either of them could have seen who did."

"I know."

"Will you ask them?"

I tapped one foot under the table while Cassia watched me, her dark eyes troubled. Her lashes were as black as her hair.

"No," I concluded.

Cassia lifted her spoon, delicately scooping up more of her broth. "Good," she said.

We finished our meal in silent understanding.

IN THE TENTH HOUR, WHEN ROME WAS BATHING, slumbering, or simply waiting for night, I took Cassia to the narrow street near the potters' area of the city, and to the door Sergius had shown me.

I'd wanted to explore alone, but as before, Cassia insisted on joining me.

She'd wrapped herself well against the sun and prying eyes and carried a canvas bag that made an occasional clinking noise. We looked like any freedman and his slave out on an errand, except that everyone knew of me, and everyone we passed watched us then turned to the nearest passerby and pointed me out.

I'd chosen the hour well though, and not many were in the hot streets to remark upon us. The lane in the Figlinae was completely deserted, shutters closed against the sun. Any person on the rare balcony high above us looked across the hills and dreamed of fresh air, paying no attention to the street below.

I found the narrow door that did not look much different from doors that led into shops and apartments. It was locked, but I nudged stones with my foot until I found a sliver of metal similar to what Sergius had used to open the other door. I inserted it into the keyhole and wriggled it about, and soon the lock clicked.

After returning the metal piece to its hiding place, I opened the door. The tunnel beyond was dark and damp, but at least it was cool.

I went in first in case another desperate man lurked, waiting to attack, but the tunnel was quiet and empty. Even the rats had decided to find someplace to sleep.

Cassia closed the door, fitting it carefully into the frame. Only then did she remove from her canvas bag the lamp and bottles of oil she'd brought. By the light from the cracks in the door, she filled the lamp and resealed the bottle, setting the lamp on the floor. My task was to light the wick.

I struck stone against stone until a spark flashed and finally caught on the twist of linen. A tiny flame began, sputtered, and then rose, bathing us in a small, golden light.

Cassia held her bag close when I reached for it, and waved for me to lead the way. What else she carried, I didn't know—Cassia had only said she'd brought things to help us in the dark.

The first part of the journey was easy, ten steps leading upward and then a straight tunnel diving back into the hill. I heard Cassia whispering behind me, counting, it sounded like.

The light showed me what the darkness had hidden

during my last journey here, that the tunnel was lined with brick, with a long, vaulted arch of cement and brick overhead to support the weight of the earth above us. Stones covered the floor, fitted into place with barely a space between them. The floor slanted inward slightly from the walls to carry any water that might accumulate down through grated drains to the sewers.

"Stop!" At Cassia's abrupt tone, I halted and swung back, ready to defend her.

Cassia was rummaging in her bag, and as I reached her, she drew out a small wooden peg and a spool of string. She tied the string to the peg and took out a wooden mallet.

"Drive this into the wall—just there." Cassia held a peg to a crack in the wall and handed me the mallet.

I secured the peg in a few short blows. Cassia unwound the string a bit, nodding at me to move on. She counted out the next twelve paces and stopped me again, holding up another peg for me to tap into the wall.

I grunted as I finished. "At this pace, we will reach Selenius's shop in maybe two days."

"If our lamp fails us and we're in the pitch dark, you'll be happy of the path I'm marking." Cassia hefted the bag over her shoulder and unwound more string. "I do not want to spend my last days lost in the sewers."

I could not argue with her logic. I'd only found my way through the tunnels with the help of Sergius and Balbus.

We went slowly along, Cassia halting me every twelve paces to secure another peg. I had to find handy cracks in the brick wall, so the string zigzagged up and down, but she was right—if we were here in the dark, we could follow the string back out, like Theseus and Ariadne in the minotaur's labyrinth.

We weren't likely to meet ancient beasts back here, only humans, rats, mildew, and filth. Bards would never sing of *our* walk through the sewers of Rome.

When we came to a junction I had to close my eyes and think very hard about how I'd come the other way. I'd been trying not to lose Sergius in the dark, not making notes of my progress.

I remembered hurrying down a slope, hoping I wouldn't have to wade through excrement from the nearest latrine. Ahead of us, one tunnel rose, and the other continued level.

"This one," I said, pointing to the rising tunnel.

Cassia studied both directions as I held up the lamp. "Are you certain?"

"No." I started into the upward sloping tunnel.

Cassia pattered behind me, halting me at the twelfth step. I tapped another peg into the wall. "Did you bring enough of these?" I asked, shouldering the mallet. "And how would you know?"

"I calculated what we need based on the distance between the two points." She gave me a nod. "I brought more than enough. Plenty of string too. We won't get lost. Don't worry."

I turned away and continued, ignoring her whispered counting behind me. She began softly singing the numbers after a time. Cassia liked to turn everything into a song.

We came upon a door, a very ordinary one—

vertical panels of wood held in place by horizontal cross pieces. I paused, holding the light to it, and Cassia stopped beside me.

"This can't be Selenius's," she said. "We haven't come far enough."

I gently pushed on the door, finding it locked. I hoped I wasn't waking a family on the other side, one with a stern paterfamilias who kept an ax and a huge guard dog.

"Selenius's door will be locked." I kept my voice quiet. "If his nephew hasn't had it bricked up yet."

"He would not have had time since we left him this morning," Cassia said, ever reasonable. "Even if his slave is taking care of it, they'd have to bring in the supplies and labor. I imagine his mother has young Gaius at home this afternoon. She was so very distressed at her brother's passing. She hasn't been well since … well, she was …" I knew Cassia could not bring herself to say the word.

Selenius's sister had been the only one who'd loved the man, it seemed. His colleagues had thought him a cheat and brute, his nephew a harsh taskmaster. But some men showed those they were fond of a different side.

"The door will still be locked," I finished. I should have brought Sergius's lock pick with me instead of returning it to its place under the stone. But I had no wish to travel back through the tunnels to fetch the piece of metal.

"No matter." Cassia reached into her bag and pulled out an iron bar, which tapered to a flat edge at the end. That explained the clanking. "You'll be able to pry it open."

I pretended to peer into the bag. "Did you bring dinner and a change of clothes as well? Perhaps a sedan chair to carry us home?"

Cassia only gave me a look and returned the pry bar to the bag. "Let us get on, shall we?"

I tramped ahead, stopping when Cassia's singing reached numbers eleven and twelve again.

In this way, we traversed the tunnels under the Esquiline Hill, circling down toward the Clivus Suburanus—I hoped.

The lamp began to sputter before we reached our destiny, and Cassia replenished its oil from the jar. More efficiency. The string was a precaution, but I doubted Cassia had not brought enough oil. She'd have calculated the exact amount needed.

Selenius's door lay at the end of a side passage—I remembered that as we rounded a corner and found a door blocking us.

There was no handle and the thing was, of course, locked, probably bolted or chained on the other side.

Cassia silently handed me the pry bar and took the lamp. I placed the tapered end of the bar in the crack between door and doorframe and pulled.

A board broke off with a loud snap. Cassia stepped back from the sudden draft that poured into the tunnel, holding her hand around the lamp's flame so it would not die.

I kept my body behind the door while I peered through the opening I'd made. The room beyond was dim, light coming through the cracks in boards over the stall window and around the ill-fitting outer door. But I recognized the cube of the room, the mosaic on the counter, the wall against which Selenius had been lolling.

My shoulders slumped in some relief. We'd reached our destination, but on the other hand, we'd found nothing in the tunnel to tell us who else had been there.

Cassia stumbled as she came to me, her bag swinging. I reached out to steady her, but she regained her feet quickly, peering down at what had made her trip.

"A loose stone," she said.

"Kick it aside," I said, wondering why she sounded so happy.

"No, no—don't you see? A loose stone *in* the floor." Cassia put her feet together and rocked back and forth on a block that moved.

"There must be many loose stones. It's an old tunnel."

"But one just *here*." Cassia waved the lamp dramatically at the floor, splashing oil. "Very convenient."

I understood her excitement, but I did not want to hope. Hope could be deadly. I crouched down and applied the pry bar to the stone.

It came up after only a few tries to reveal a cavity beneath. Cassia dropped to her knees and peered inside with interest, then set down the lamp and started to reach into the hole.

"Wait!" I stopped her—who knew what would crawl out of such a place? I thrust the iron bar into the space and lifted out a bundle of cloth, which clattered when I dropped it to the tunnel floor.

Cassia tore open the knots that held the bundle closed and spread out the cloth.

We stared down at a garment that had been splashed heavily with blood, now dried and brown. A thin-bladed knife rested in the middle of the linen, blackened with the same gore.

CHAPTER 11

NEITHER OF US SPOKE AS WE GAZED AT THE bloodstained clothes and knife.

The man had stood in front of his victim, I decided. The tunic was splashed from neck to hem in a spray that would have come from the throat when it was cut. If the killer had stood behind Selenius, Selenius's body would have blocked most of the blood.

Cassia put her hand to her mouth and made a soft gagging sound.

"Selenius knew his killer," I said calmly. "Trusted him."

"How do you know that?" Cassia asked through her fingers.

"He didn't fight," I said, remembering the body slumped under the counter. "His hands were unmarred." They'd held no bruises or abrasions from Selenius trying to hit his killer.

"You mean he did not expect the person to attack him." Cassia swallowed as she looked back down at the cloth. "This tunic is far too big to fit Sergius." Her words held relief, and the same relief coursed through me.

"But not Balbus." I calculated the garment's dimensions. "This was made for a thin man."

I'd be sorry if Balbus had done this. He hadn't struck me as being evil, in spite of his attack on me. He was desperate and terrified, as any runaway slave would be. If he'd killed Selenius it would have been to save himself.

"Balbus was carrying a knife when he tried to stab you," Cassia reminded me. "The killer discarded this one. And Balbus never wore this tunic." She gingerly lifted an unstained part of the hem. "This is expensive linen, finely woven, the stitches precise and strong. This was made by a good tailor, and not long ago. It's not worn enough to have been bought secondhand, though I grant it might have been stolen."

Tunics and other clothing were stolen from laundries all the time, the thieves then selling the garments for a nice sum.

"The killer brought a change of clothing with him?" I asked doubtfully. "Meaning he knew the murder could get messy?" I shook my head. "No. This wasn't planned. The two men began to argue, one caught up a knife—"

"And already had a change of clothing ready," Cassia said. "Because he comes to this shop often."

We looked at each other. I read sadness in her expression, pity, and regret.

"We don't have to tell anyone," I pointed out. "We

can put the tunic and knife back. No one has found it but us—who else would look?"

"But the magistrates will go on hunting Balbus," Cassia returned. "If he's found, he'll be thrown to the lions. Or they'll come for *you*. No, Leonidas, we have to report this. We have laws for a reason."

I tasted bitterness. "Your same law would see Balbus torn apart, or me sent to the games for a crime I didn't commit. It saw you taken from the home you'd known all your life and sent to serve a gladiator who was supposed to have broken you."

Cassia swallowed. "I know. But …"

I grabbed the tunic and knife, rolled the cloth into a ball, and stuffed it into the canvas bag Cassia had let slide to the floor. I took up the pry bar and climbed to my feet.

"We'll take these out," I said. "Burn them, throw them into the river, I don't care. Maybe you can talk me around by the time we get out of the tunnels, and I'll take them to a praetor instead—but I don't know."

The fact that Cassia didn't argue with me but only rose, took up the lamp, and followed told me much. She didn't want to cause Selenius's family more tragedy either.

I had to concede she was correct in part—a killer couldn't simply cut down men whenever he was angry with them. If he did it once and got away with it, there was nothing to stop him doing it again.

But I'd have the entire journey through the tunnels to think about it. I would put off the decision until we emerged into the light of day—or dusk, which it must be by now.

My mistake was in letting Cassia walk behind me. Not until she cried out did I understand how foolish I'd been to think us in no danger.

I turned. He held Cassia around the waist, a knife pressed to her throat. The hilt of the knife glittered softly in the light of the dropped lamp flickering at Cassia's feet, her dark curls sliding free of her palla to frame her terrified face.

My numbness fled. Rage like molten iron burned through my blood, clashing with the freezing dread at the image of Cassia falling, her throat slit, my Cassia dead before me.

I dropped the bag but hefted the pry bar, the fighting man in me ready to strike at my enemy.

"I like her," young Gaius Selenius said, tears in his voice. "She was so kind to my mother. I don't want to hurt her."

I wasn't certain whether he meant Cassia or his mother in his last declaration, but it didn't matter.

A few moments ago, I'd been ready to hide the crime and let Gaius go. He'd rid himself of an uncle who'd been a fraud and beaten him whenever he'd liked, and I suspected worse besides.

But if Gaius harmed Cassia I would kill him. He'd die, and then I would. It would be a tragedy worthy of any dramatist.

"Let her go," I snapped. "You can flee Rome—your mother can too. I'll destroy the clothes and knife. We'll let the magistrates think a passing madman killed your uncle."

Gaius shook his head, but the knife didn't waver from Cassia's throat. "I heard you talking. *She* wants to

have me arrested." His arm tightened on Cassia's
waist.

Cassia spoke rapidly, her voice shaking. "Leonidas
is a trained killer, Gaius. You'll never escape him."

"I don't care." Gaius's words were petulant. "I'll
fight him — he can kill me. I'll die honorably, in a battle
with you as witness."

"No," I said in hard tones. If I killed a man of the
merchant class, though he was a murderer himself, I'd
likely not be granted the dignity of dying in the games.
They might crucify me instead, just to set an example.

But if he didn't let go of Cassia, I'd break his neck
and dump his body into the Tiber.

"He must have been awful," Cassia said to Gaius.
"We heard that he ill-used you. And if his fraud were
discovered, it would go badly for you and your
mother."

"I care nothing for that!" Gaius cried, his voice
rising again. "I could take his beatings. His dishonesty
at least made us money. I killed him because he
touched *her*. He is supposed to protect her, and he did
the worst thing a man could do to a woman — especially
his *sister*. And *still* she loved him."

Cassia's brief intake of breath sounded loud in the
stillness. "Oh, Gaius, no. I'm so sorry."

He had a knife to her throat, nothing to keep him
from slicing her as he had his uncle, and Cassia felt
sorry for him.

Gaius had just confirmed my suspicions that Selenius had been more than simply a brute and a trickster.
I remembered how the young man in the baths had
told me Selenius's sister had been violated by one of

Selenius's friends. That was likely what the rumor had become when the gossip spread from the house. The truth, I realized now, was more terrible than that.

I recalled Cassia's mention of her visit to Gaius and his mother Selenia, how upset Selenia had been at her brother's death. Perhaps not because she'd loved her brother and he'd been murdered, but because she'd realized her son killed him, and she knew why.

Gaius had nearly broken into tears when he'd told us Selenius been a father to him. A father who had done such a horrible thing to his mother.

"He raped her," I said, the blatant word ugly. "You couldn't stop him."

Tears ran down Gaius's face. "He said it was her duty to be with him. He dishonored her and violated her—his own *sister*. She wouldn't let me accuse him, wouldn't let me make him pay for what he'd done. Wouldn't let me bring shame on the family." Gaius hiccupped air. "That day … that morning … I was doing his bidding as usual. He and my mother had argued before we'd come, and he'd beaten her to the floor. While we were here, he began to taunt me. Said he'd had whores far better than my mother, that she was weak and stupid and had born a weak and stupid son. He'd laid his knife on the counter. No one was outside. I grabbed it—I don't know what I meant to do. But then I was swinging it at his throat. It went right through." Gaius gulped and the knife came too close to nicking Cassia's skin. "I had to do it. I had to avenge her."

"I know," I said, feeling sick. "I would have done the same. But Cassia has not harmed you. Let her go, or you will die. Painfully. I won't let you fight back, and so you'll have no honor, and I'll throw away your body. Your mother will always wonder what happened to you."

Cassia's alarm grew, not for herself but for me. But I couldn't halt my tongue. If young Gaius hurt Cassia, I'd pull off his arms and roll his torso along to an opening of the sewers, flushing him away with the rest of Rome's refuse.

Gaius sobbed now, clinging to Cassia as though loath to release her. His eyes closed tightly with his tears, and he turned his head.

Two steps took me to him. One squeeze of my fist broke the hand that held the knife. Gaius screamed, trying to fight, but too late.

I had him on the ground, his arm twisted behind him, my foot on his skinny thighs. I held the iron pry bar to his throat.

"A gladiator stabs, he doesn't slice," I said in a harsh voice. "More likely to make a hit, and death is quicker."

Gaius continued to wail and sob. Cassia picked up the knife, holding it loosely in one hand, as I'd taught her, but she had to brace herself on the wall with the other, her breath ragged.

I lifted the pry bar, drew back my foot, and kicked Gaius in the head. He went limp, and mercifully, the sounds pouring from his mouth ceased.

I WAITED IN SELENIUS'S CLOSED SHOP, GAIUS

slumped under the counter where his uncle had died, while Cassia went to fetch his mother.

At Cassia's insistence, I relinquished the bloody clothes and knife to her. What she'd do with them, I didn't know, and I did not ask.

I knew she was canny enough not to walk into Selenia's house and announce we'd captured her son, so I did not worry about her going by herself on her errand. She'd persuade Gaius's mother to come, and come alone.

I sat on the floor, though a perfectly good stool reposed near the cupboard. I leaned my head against the wall and closed my eyes, trying to let the silence of the place calm me.

Gaius was tied with strips torn from his bloody tunic — even if he woke, he'd not be attacking me. We'd searched him for more weapons, but he'd had none.

He'd likely been returning at this quiet hour, as we had, to retrieve the tunic and knife from under the stone. Yesterday, this shop had been alive with cohorts, the other shopkeepers, and gawpers. Today would have been his first chance to return unnoticed. We'd been right to search the tunnels as soon as we could.

Gaius had likely kept a change of clothing here, in the cupboard perhaps, in case his uncle had him work through the night, or perhaps he simply didn't like wearing anything dirty.

I didn't know what would become of Gaius and his mother, and I was no longer interested. I could prove now that I didn't kill Selenius, and that Balbus hadn't either, but that wasn't what relieved me.

I'd been imagining, awake and asleep, the child

Sergius, having been frightened by Selenius, slashing out with the knife and killing the man. Or creeping up on him and doing the same.

Sergius was the small, innocent boy I'd been before life had made me otherwise. I'd later been labeled a killer, and sent to the games where I could murder for other people's entertainment.

No more killing, I'd vowed the day I'd gained my freedom and the *rudis*, the wooden sword that symbolized it. And yet, murder followed me.

I couldn't keep myself from death. But I could save Sergius from it, and Cassia.

Cassia arrived with Selenia in tow. Only Cassia and Selenia entered the shop, so Cassia must have persuaded her to leave the litter bearers and maids outside in the street. She couldn't have stopped Selenia from bringing servants altogether—a Roman matron did not hurry through the streets on foot and alone.

I kept my eyes closed and the cold wall behind me as Selenia cried out upon seeing her son. Cassia explained to Selenia what had happened, and Selenia broke down, Cassia comforting her.

They could leave Rome, Cassia said. "No one will question that you wanted to go far from the place of your brother's death," she went on, her voice soothing. "Take your son and go. We will say nothing."

"He didn't mean to be cruel," Selenia replied brokenly. I wondered whether she meant her son or her brother. "Yes, I'll take Gaius far away." She drew a sobbing breath. "I have your word?"

"You have our word," Cassia reassured her.

The word of a slave and a gladiator should count

for nothing. We weren't people to most. I was marginally a person now that I'd been freed, but only just.

But Cassia had a way with her. I opened my eyes a crack to see the matron swathed in her silks from the East hugging Cassia and crying.

I rose at long last, lifted the unconscious Gaius over my shoulder, and trudged through the deserted shops to the dark street. I loaded him into Selenia's litter then helped her in behind him. It was Cassia who gave the order for the litter bearers to start down the street, the maids trotting along after it.

I took Cassia's hand and led her home.

❧

TWO DAYS LATER, WE LEFT ROME AND WENT ALONG the Via Appia to the Via Latina. Cassia was perched on a donkey, Sergius's precious cup wrapped in a bundle before her.

I led the donkey—the beast had been my idea, although Cassia had insisted she'd be able to walk the five miles to Marcella's farm. I knew she couldn't and pointed out that she'd pay for her pride by having to travel the last part of the distance slung over my shoulder. That argument had convinced Cassia to pay the few coins for the donkey.

We shared a loaf of Quintus's bread as we went along, Cassia chattering to me. She could find enough to talk about to fill a five-mile journey and have plenty left over.

She told me that Selenia and Gaius had left the city early this morning, heading for a house Selenia had inherited in the north, near Tuscana. Cassia had heard this from servants of Selenia's household—the family would sell the business and turn to growing wine or some such thing.

Cassia hadn't left our apartment since we'd returned from sending Gaius and Selenia home, but Cassia, through the vast number of acquaintances she'd made since coming to me, could discover what happened at the far end of town without stirring a step.

Cassia had found out—through these same connections—how I'd had to pay for my dinner at the tavern in the Pallacinae. She'd not said so directly, but she'd made a show of putting extra coins in my purse, saying I'd not be caught without them again. Other than that, she never mentioned the matter.

Now Cassia turned her face to the sun, what bit of it she let show from behind her draped wrap. "How lovely to be in the open air again." She let out a happy breath. "There's no place more beautiful than Campania, Leonidas. We'll go there sometime."

I only made a neutral noise. Traveling cost money, and who knew how far our benefactor would let us out of his sight?

For now, it was enough that we could breathe air that held none of the smoke and stenches of the city, that the sun shone warm and the breeze was cool. The men in Rome would hunt a foreign slave for a murder and then give up when they couldn't find Balbus, safe in his disguise in the ludus. Selenius's shop would be taken over by another money-changer, and the man's death would be forgotten.

We'd give Sergius back his cup with my name on it,

eat Marcella's hearty food, and curl up for the night in the warmth of her barn. Then back to Rome to exist a while longer.

"You'll have to take another job when we return," Cassia said around a bite of bread. "A loaf a day is all very well, but that will end in time, and our coffers are fearsomely low."

"They always are," I muttered.

Cassia pretended not to hear me. "Perhaps you could guard someone all the way to Neapolis," she said. "It's lovely there, across the bay from Herculaneum. Beauty you've never seen, Leonidas."

"I *have* seen it," I answered. "I was hired out for games there, years ago."

"Oh." She sounded a bit disappointed, then brightened. "Then you would see it again, but this time we could wander the streets and eat in the best taverns, and climb the hills for the view. Delightful."

"Delightful," I repeated. "When I look for this job, I'll make sure the employer knows it must be delightful."

"You are making fun of me, Leonidas."

"Yes." I kept my face straight. "Or we can return to Rome, and I can sleep." I was already tired, longing to reach Marcella's where I could lie on straw and close my eyes. Cassia and Marcella would talk—and talk—and I'd lie back and let their voices drift over me.

"You are always sleeping, Leonidas," Cassia said without rancor. "One day, you will have to wake up."

"One day, I will," I said.

"I have your word?"

"You do." I might be *infamis*, but I honored my promises, and Cassia knew it.

"That's all right then." Cassia turned her face to the road.

Before long, she started to hum, a clear tune she liked. In another few yards, she was softly singing.

The words flowed around me to be caught by the breeze and rise into the clear blue sky.

AUTHOR'S NOTE

THANK YOU FOR READING! I HOPE YOU ENJOYED this glimpse of the new Leonidas the Gladiator Mysteries.

As you might guess, while this is the first offering in the series, it will not be Book One. The first novel will introduce Leonidas and Cassia and show how they came to know and depend on each other. I'll go into more detail about the characters' backgrounds, the mysterious benefactor, and how Leonidas begins to solve crimes.

I don't know at the moment when that book will be finished—please check my website: www.gardnermysteries.com or sign up for my newsletter at http://eepurl.com/5n7rz to be notified when it is ready for pre-order and released.

If a vegetarian gladiator surprises you, archaeologists have discovered, by studying the bones of gladiators and other athletes, that their diet consisted mostly of vegetables, with a little starch, like barley and beans, to supplement it. Gladiators were fed the best foods available, as the more robust a man was, the better he performed and the more money could be made from him. Gladiators also had regular massages after their training and the best physicians to look after them.

I will explore more about the gladiators' world and more of Rome in the time of Nero in the novels.

When picturing the Rome of Nero, we have to erase from the city much of what we think of as "Roman" (e.g., the Coliseum, Trajan's column, the Pantheon as we see it today, and more) — these were great building projects of the later first and early second centuries AD (Hadrian rebuilt Agrippa's Pantheon, though he left Agrippa's name on the portico). We must imagine Rome before the fire of AD 64, when warrens of streets were wrapped with wooden and stone buildings.

Among my research materials for this era, I found mapping projects of early first-century Rome, which helped me follow Leonidas about the streets, and a fascinating digital reconstruction of Nero's Domus Aurea (Golden House), which did not exist at the time of this story, but will come into future novels.

Again, I hope you enjoyed a look into Leonidas's world. More to come!

All my best,

Ashley Gardner

ALSO BY ASHLEY GARDNER

Leonidas the Gladiator Mysteries

Blood Debts

(More to come)

Kat Holloway Victorian Mysteries Series

A Soupçon of Poison

Death Below Stairs

Scandal Above Stairs

Captain Lacey Regency Mystery Series

The Hanover Square Affair

A Regimental Murder

The Glass House

The Sudbury School Murders

The Necklace Affair

(in print in

The Necklace Affair and Other Stories)

A Body in Berkeley Square

A Covent Garden Mystery

A Death in Norfolk

A Disappearance in Drury Lane

Murder in Grosvenor Square

The Thames River Murders

The Alexandria Affair

A Mystery at Carlton House

The Gentleman's Walking Stick

(short stories: in print in

The Necklace Affair and Other Stories)

Captain Lacey Regency Mysteries, Vol 1

Includes

The Hanover Square Affair

A Regimental Murder

The Glass House

The Gentleman's Walking Stick

(short story collection)

Captain Lacey Regency Mysteries, Vol 2

Includes

The Sudbury School Murders

The Necklace Affair

A Body in Berkeley Square

A Covent Garden Mystery

Captain Lacey Regency Mysteries, Vol 3

Includes